SWEET, SEXY, SCANDALOUS

THE COMPLETE SERIES

IDA BRADY

Cover design by Christine's Cover Creations

Formatting by Ebony McKenna

www.idabrady.com

To Team Brida,
For all the love, support and chocolate.

To Tango, with Love,
Where it all began.

SWEET SPOT

SWEET, SEXY, SCANDALOUS BOOK 1

A Sweet, Sexy, Scandalous Series

Sweet
SPOT

~ BOOK ONE ~

IDA BRADY

CHAPTER ONE

AT TWENTY-FIVE, AMIRA HADID WAS MORE THAN EAGER to have her cherry popped.

Which was kind of hard to do when she still lived with her ultraconservative parents.

Parents who viewed every guy they hadn't approved as a threat to her chastity. Not that the family home was an ideal place for wild, debauched sex parties. Or even tame ones for that matter. But as they *still* thought it was acceptable to walk into her room without knocking, she figured bringing a guy home for a sexy romp wouldn't exactly be a private affair.

Because of this, Amira had become adept at leading a double life: dutiful daughter and seamstress by day, tango and sex addict by night.

Though, perhaps she had to *have* sex first before she qualified for that title.

Except she didn't want sex with just any man. She may have been a virgin in heat, but she was a picky one. And until Mr. Great Sex came along, she would have to live with her virgin status a little while longer.

Stepping over the slick cobblestones, Amira rolled her shoulders, stiff after a long day at work. She had stayed back late, again, after her current Bridezilla demanded even more alterations on her dress. If she had to sew one more bead on that hem, Miss It's My Day would surely topple over.

She weaved in and out of alleyways passing many of the hidden clubs, cocktail lounges, and dance halls nestled in Melbourne's CBD. By the end of the week, Amira was eager for a man's touch. This Thursday proved no different.

Tango was a release. Not necessarily the one she was after, but a way to rid herself of the heavy weight of duty that dogged her waking hours. Though lately, dancing the Argentine tango seemed to heighten her desire for something…

Not a relationship exactly. Not a fuck buddy either.

A lover.

She savored the word on her tongue.

Yes, a lover. Where there would be an exchange of intimacy, affection and smoking hot sex. She bit her lip to stop the fanciful grin; she was used to hiding her thoughts from others.

When she finally got the money and the courage to move out, she would buy an apartment in the city. Not just any apartment. She had her eye on one of the stunning Art Deco designed buildings, a relic of the old Melbourne quarter. The three-story building was nestled in the heart of Collins Street; known for fashion, food and fucking hot men in suits.

Once that apartment was hers, she would address her virgin status. And dismantle it like a demolition worker at a construction site—with unbridled gusto and carefree abandon.

Naturally, Amira blamed her parents for her current sexless status. She had been deprived of men for too long. Her hunger for sex was like the air surrounding her, heavy and close. Demanding to be satisfied.

She had an all-consuming need to be filled. She woke up with it, showered with it, went to bed every single night, unsatisfied with it. The yearning accompanied her every hour; a throbbing, heady drum beat that echoed through her body reminding her of what was missing. It had started when she turned eighteen and only increased in fervor with every passing year.

But only a skilled lover would do. A man who knew his way around a woman's body, someone who could give the sort of gratification she sought in her dreams.

The image of such a man flitted through her mind. Tall, dark, handsome. And a stranger.

Amira slid back the unmarked industrial door that led to the dance hall and wondered if she would see *him* again tonight.

For a year it was the same. At exactly 10pm every Thursday, he would arrive at the *milonga*. And she would know, whether she was dancing with someone else, or sitting at one of the circular tables at the edges of the dance floor, that he was watching. She would feel a delicious shiver at the nape of her neck and know it was him.

The foreplay was driving her wild.

While her university days had been filled with endless hours of dressmaking designs, patterns and prints, her friends had been boozing and bonking to the wee hours. But she had craved more.

Somehow, she knew that he would be the answer the moment she spotted him in the shadows of the *milonga*.

"Amira, welcome."

"Hey, Gus." She bent down to kiss the portly *tanguero* on the cheek. A strong, pungent aftershave hit her, as did the cigarette smoke. No matter how much cologne he wore, or how many extra-strong mints he consumed, she could always smell the Marlboro on him. It was both comforting and repelling.

She paid the entrance fee and took off her coat. The lesson had ended and the *milonga*—the evening of social dancing—was just beginning. A few dancers she knew were warming up or socializing.

Taking her time, Amira found a table and slipped on her tango shoes. She surreptitiously scanned the rectangular room once more. The space was large but empty enough for her to take stock. As she did, an elderly gentleman approached.

"Edward." Amira smiled, warming when the septuagenarian bowed. Whilst dancing with him was more akin to stilted bouts of walking around the floor, she enjoyed his gentle embrace and lively conversation.

"My Amira. Care to dance with an old fool?"

"You're neither, Ed, as you well know. I'd be delighted."

They danced in an open embrace, chests apart, movements slow, but it was the camaraderie, the shared understanding between them that made the connection unique, one steeped in affection and respect. She had learned more about life than tango from Ed, and that in itself was good enough.

Thanks to her parents, her interaction with men was minimal. Functional at best.

Taking lessons with Alejandro and Tilda had been one of the few places she had a chance to mingle with the opposite sex. She was able to form friendships with straight men for the first time since graduating university. All the male friends she had acquired through fashion school were gay. Lovely, handsome men, but not at all interested in de-flowering her.

"Your dancing is divine, Amira. Why are you wasting your talents on boring men like me?"

She completed a *giro*, turning slowly, allowing his back to make the necessary adjustments.

"You're a treasure, Edward. I happen to enjoy our dances together."

"As do I. But maybe in time another man will catch your eye and your heart. And you can find yourself a true partner, your equal. Like I did my Penny."

Edward's tale of his much-loved wife surrounded her. They had met at a tango lesson when both were shy of eighteen. Back then dancing tango was still a past time that was kept behind closed doors. They had married two months later and stayed that way until her death five years ago.

"Find a man who can dance, Amira, and your heart will shine as bright as the moon. Trust me, men don't like to share their love. Or their women. Especially when you dance the way you do. An angel!"

Laughing, she guided him back to his table once the set was over. Her desire to improve had been driven by the dark, assessing gaze of a man she didn't even know.

No sooner had she sat down that another dancer approached.

When supper was served a few hours later, Amira stood back and scanned the crowd yet again. She looked at the clock at the far end of the hall. It was past 10. He still hadn't arrived.

Leaving her untouched supper on the table, Amira

accepted Gus' offer to dance, grateful for the distraction. The barrel-chested man was always jolly, and tonight was no different.

"Aaamiiiiiraaaaa," he sang. "Did you know there was a song about a beautiful princess called Amira? It was before your time." He chuckled, swinging her around in his arms.

"You tell me this every time we dance, Gus."

"Ah, I'm old. I can't remember."

She adjusted her center, given that he was a good head shorter. When a *vals tanda* came on, she breathed a small sigh of relief. Dancing a *milonga* with Gus was a health and safety violation. The man only knew one speed. Fast.

Vals or not, he was still a whirlwind. She caught brief glimpses of other dancers before concentrating on maintaining her axis. With some men she could float across the floor, lost in the embrace, but with Gus she maintained her vigilance.

"There's a sadness in you." He narrowed his eyes.

Amira shook her head. "No sadness."

"No? You calling ol' Gus a liar? I see it in those pretty brown eyes."

With every step around the floor, Amira's heart sank. She didn't want to think about returning home. To her parents' home. Alone. That she still lived with them was embarrassing enough, but at twenty-five, not having a boyfriend was just plain sad. Even in her parents' culture, she should have been married by now.

She repressed a shudder. A dutiful marriage was her idea of hell.

She didn't want to return home to another cold—

Her heart slammed in her ribs. The familiar spread of fire burned through her body, fanning out against her cheeks.

A pair of dark, assessing eyes caught her own.

The joy radiated through her, a lone candle in the dark night. Suddenly alive and deliriously happy, Amira fought to control her breathing. But with each rotation around the floor, their eyes met. Watching *him*, watch *her*, had heightened her arousal.

He was immaculate in a dark suit and crisp white shirt. His tanned skin spoke of Mediterranean seas, of sandy Arabian deserts. Of desire.

A woman approached, flirtatious and adoring, yet he remained stoic. Not once did he break eye contact with her. Noticing this, the woman left.

Everything else faded, where he remained in sharp contrast.

Whilst his direct gaze was intimate, it was her response to him that fuelled her fantasies. *This* was what she had been longing for ever since she had turned eighteen and felt there was something missing from her pleasure. Since that sledge-hammer of lust had blown through her defenses and left her shuddering and straining for something more than her fingers.

The song was coming to an end, and her focus redirected to Gus as he stepped back and began peppering her with questions. Amira could barely hear him over the rushing in her ears.

She didn't dare look in the corner where *he* was standing. Not until she had regained her composure. A few minutes later when she did, she was surprised to see the space was vacant. Amira searched through the crowds, on the dance floor and at the end of the hall, but failed to find the enigmatic stranger.

He had simply vanished.

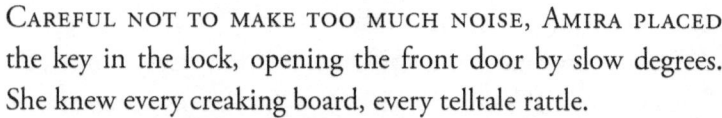

CAREFUL NOT TO MAKE TOO MUCH NOISE, AMIRA PLACED the key in the lock, opening the front door by slow degrees. She knew every creaking board, every telltale rattle.

This was why she had to find a place of her own and move out. She was sick of sneaking in like she was some adolescent and not a fully grown adult. Not that her parents would ever see her that way. In their eyes, she was some innocent in need of shelter from the big bad world.

But Amira craved big. She was intrigued by bad. And something told her *he* was definitely a man of the world.

If her parents only knew what their youngest daughter was thinking, she'd be locked away for life. Which was another problem. Bringing men home was a no-no. Bringing them home for wild, debauched sex would probably result in being disowned.

She had been taught from a young age that sex before marriage was a sin. Disobeying her parents would be inevitable, and at some stage, when she had saved up enough so she'd never have to move back, it would be painful. But when she left, it wouldn't be because she was married to some man her parents approved. It would be because she was able to support herself. Regardless of duty.

She was her own woman. One who was almost dizzy with the need for release.

"'Mira, is that you?" Her mother's sleepy voice rang through from the bedroom.

"Yes, go to back to bed," she whispered.

But she knew her mother rarely slept until she was home. It was stressful at the best of times. Suffocating at the worst.

"Where have you been?"

"We'll talk in the morning. Goodnight."

Amira tiptoed up the stairs and down the hall to the back of the house. She waited until she heard her mother's telltale snoring before sneaking to the bathroom. She could never be too certain that she wasn't followed for a late-night grilling. It had happened before.

She locked the door, then turned on the shower. Stripping off her clothes, she stepped under the spray, closing the screen door behind her. The minute the water hit her body, the tension she had been carrying began to ebb away.

Everything was muted except the pulsing at her core. Picking up the shower head, she ran the nozzle over her face, then slowly down her breasts. She played with the intensity of the spray until she found the right pressure. She wanted to toy with herself, to extend that moment of release until only her satisfaction mattered.

When she closed her eyes, she saw *him*. Always him. Watching her dance, following her every move.

His mouth on her neck, biting, sucking until she couldn't breathe. That body—firm and solid—pressing, demanding, against hers.

She stroked herself now, allowing her imagination free reign. Straddling him, she guided his hard length inside her.

Her hips strained. She pinched her nipples with one hand and lowered the nozzle to the thatch of auburn curls between her thighs. Amira jerked. Every nerve was alive, eager and straining for direct contact.

She pictured him now kneeling between her thighs, his tongue working over her, lapping at her wet core, gripping her hips. She wanted to feel those fingers biting into her ass, holding her in place. She jerked back and forth as the pressure of the shower head beat down.

Amira dipped one finger inside, just the tip, until she felt pressure, and a pinching sensation. She inched back, pressing her knuckles against her entrance with one hand, with the other she directed the nozzle against her clit.

"Yes."

Tipping back her head, she bucked her hips back and forth, ribbons of pleasure winding tighter and tighter, wrapping around her until she trembled.

He watched her now, pleasuring herself. Amira stretched her legs further apart, adjusting the pressure. She wanted to draw out her orgasm, but every time she directed the water to her clit, her legs began to shake.

Every time she pictured *him*, sucking her, fucking her, she almost lost control.

Bouncing up and down on the nozzle, Amira pinched her nipples. His mouth on her breasts. His cock inside of her, pounding away as she straddled his hips.

And then it happened, the build-up reached an exquisite level of intensity. She crested at the peak, gasping, breaking into a million fragmented pieces. Cupping her sex, she ground back against her fingers, riding her orgasm until she was no longer shaking.

Still, he watched her.

But her body was spent, her arms heavy. She shook off the alluring images, mind fatigued. Once would have to do for tonight. Amira finished showering and ignored the tingling sensation of the towel on her body as she dried off.

Her nighttime routine complete, she tiptoed back to her bedroom, closing the door and climbing into bed. Alone.

His face swam into view the minute she closed her eyes. Almost instantly, she slept.

CHAPTER TWO

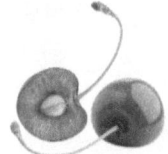

Amira stretched out her overused muscles, massaging her hands to release the cramping. After a busy weekend of sketching and sewing, she was grateful to have an evening out of the house.

Three years ago, she would never have imagined she would be plotting how to start her own freelance business, and certainly not tango dresses of all things.

But when she had worn one of her tango skirts to class that sunny spring day, she wouldn't have believed it could change her life. The design had been one born out of her own curiosity and her research of famous tango dancers. The end result had been a skirt that was playful and daring, and one her dance teacher, Tilda, had noticed the moment she stepped foot in the studio.

What had become a small passion project had turned into a freelance job, designing tango clothes for Tilda's performances. Work that would make moving out an actual reality.

Her heart danced. Now her dresses would be on show at the *Mundial de Tango* for all the world to see. Her designs. Her ideas. It was Tilda's enthusiasm that gave her the confidence to try out new patterns and prints, which led to interest from other dancers wanting custom made designs. She would have to carve out some time over the next few months to create a website showcasing her work. If she wanted to progress in this career, she had to take those chances, calculate the risks.

Afraid she would jinx it if she thought too much about her future, Amira gave a quick tap on the wooden railing, and emerged from the underground train station into the heavy rain. Her sequined, pastel skirt fanned out as she raced across the busy intersection. The slit at the thigh wasn't very revealing, but for a woman who dressed modestly most of the time, she felt wonderfully on display. It had been a daring, bold choice, but she made it with one aim in mind: to shine.

Tonight's *milonga* at Bentleigh Place gave her the perfect excuse to wear it. The monthly gathering attracted great dancers from across the city. The international guest teachers always drew a crowd, and Amira was lucky to have booked a spot. It was a workshop about connections after all. She hadn't been able to resist.

Stepping out of the wet, she entered the old brick building. The narrow entrance was already lined with people. Worming through the crowd, Amira squeezed into a spot at the back of the room, leaning on the exposed brick wall to buckle the strap of her shoes.

There was a steady, sensual pulse to Bentleigh Place. It reverberated through her body, heightening her anticipation.

Before taking lessons in tango, she had never had a man's hands on her waist. Before taking lessons, she had never appreciated the male form; the confines of their embrace, some playful, others powerful, marked a quality specific to the dancer. It was this difference that teased out new elements of her own dancing. It was what made tango a dance of surprises.

She tucked a damp wisp of hair behind her ear, ignoring the shiver that tickled her spine.

Tonight's lesson was about maintaining the connection between the lead and follower. It was the most basic aspect of tango, but the most crucial. The connection, the trust shared between two people in an embrace was as tender as a kiss. It was through this that all communication occurred. Was it any wonder she was hooked?

When the Argentinian teachers began the lesson, a hush settled across the room.

They started with a series of warm-up drills, splitting the floor in two groups. Even with the cool night, Amira's body was on fire. Too many people, not enough air.

"Connection with your partner is key," the Argentinian stated, pacing the floor. "Without it, you are hollow and your movement meaningless. Maintaining the connection is a basic and fundamental component when engaging with your partner. Gentlemen, I want you to form a circle around the room and raise your arms as if you were embracing an imaginary person. *Bueno*. Excellent.

"Now close your eyes."

A low murmur ensued, some men coughing in nervous anticipation, others laughing. Every man was exposed, vulnerable.

"Ladies, it's your turn. Find a man. Position yourself in the empty space of your partner's arms. It is not simply our job as leaders to initiate that bond. Remember that as a follower you are just as responsible. You are both leaders and followers in that sense. As a couple, you must create and maintain that connection until I ask you to rotate."

Beyond the brick walls of Bentleigh Place, she heard the rain lashing against the cars and buildings, marking its own rhythm. Amira smoothed down her skirt and turned. A man her age whom she had danced with before shifted from one foot to the other, waiting for a partner. His eye lids fluttered; his arms were half raised. She recalled that he worked in IT and had once revealed that he took lessons to improve his confidence with women. But his name escaped her.

When she moved into his open arms, he stiffened. Oftentimes he had requested to dance in an open embrace, chests apart. It seemed he had yet to grow out of his discomfort. She inwardly applauded his gumption, even if she didn't agree.

She yearned for that moment of connection with a partner, looked forward to it with every dance. Sharing that space was a vital part of tango. Bodily contact was essential.

As the minutes shifted by, his regimented stance began to crumble. His touch, where once stiff, was now soft. His breathing easy. She smiled at his satisfied sigh. He had found it. Accepted it. A new milestone.

After a series of drills, the women swapped circles. Unable to find a partner, Amira stepped to the side only to have the Argentine teacher direct her to a lone figure at the far end of the room.

A shot of adrenaline pumped through her. She tried to regulate her breathing, shocked that *he* was here. At the nudge on her shoulder, she stepped forward. All the men still had their eyes closed, waiting for their partners to step into their embrace. Including *him*.

Her heart galloped, the expectation of dancing with him

coursing through her veins. For months she had wondered whether they would be compatible as dancers. Lovers. Now she would find out.

Taking a deep breath, Amira slipped in between the gap of his raised arms and studied his face. She had the luxury of admiring the line of his jaw, the sweep of dark lashes before gently leaning forward, keeping her back straight as she pressed her chest against his. She was immediately surrounded by his scent. Cinnamon and leather and something more. An elemental fragrance, compelling, intoxicating.

His arm circled around her, adjusted and settled. She was overcome by the hard muscle against her breasts, by the firm hold across her waist.

Her body vibrated like a plucked violin string.

She placed her right hand in his raised left and rested her right temple to his cheek, completing the embrace. His breath caressed the base of her neck, fanning the fire, scorching her skin. What she would give to be out of this room, out of her clothes. With him.

Amira adjusted her stance so that her frame was locked, and all her weight rested on her left heel. The loneliness that pervaded her waking hours seemed to dissipate. This man, this stranger whom she did not know, called to her on a primordial level. She attempted to relax her shoulders, to regulate her breathing, but it was as if she were drowning in him.

His hands cupping her ass.

His mouth—demanding—at her nipples.

Little shocks rippled over her breasts.

Oh yes, she could picture what sex with this dark-haired stranger would be like. How he would devour her, driving her to the edge and then over, again and again. She trembled, mouth parched.

The Argentinian's voice floated behind her. "It is important that you both feel that connection. You should feel the pressure of your chest in contact with your partner, such that if the gentlemen stepped forward, ladies, you would move accordingly. Remember you are responding to the music as one."

Her nipples pebbled against his body and a delicate shiver traipsed down her back. There was almost an erotic quality to being able to see when her partner could not.

The connection was effortless, intimate.

They shifted weight from one foot to the other, executing simple turns, all the while their chests pressed together, their bodies moving as one. Amira was overcome. By him. By her need for a man. By the luxury of another's touch.

She held her back straight when all she wanted was to sink against him. Lulled into the rhythm, she glided, barely listening to the instructions from the teachers. Her sole focus was the mysterious stranger whom she fantasized about for so long now.

"Whoever you are, you have a beautiful embrace." The timber of his voice vibrated through her chest. It was deep, smooth. A flush crept over her face. She lapped up his words, savoring them and her response.

Amira cleared her throat. "I could say the same of you."

His eyes flashed open, a dark and deep brown. Surprise and appreciation dawned across his face. He lingered on her lips, heating her skin.

She stared back. Afraid it was a dream. Afraid to break the connection.

"I knew you would have this…"

"What?"

He weighed his words, pausing. "Sensuality. There is something about the way you move that draws people to you."

"Just people?"

She was emboldened by his words. She was another woman in his arms.

They swayed, shifting the weight from one foot to the other. He kept a small space between them, leading as per the Argentine's instructions. His gaze lowered, leaving a trail of embers scattered across her breasts until it hovered above her panties, setting her alight.

"Me. You intrigue me, Amira. As you do countless other men. Social dancing has refined your technique. I've made it a point to study you."

"Study me?"

"I've watched your progress…but then you know that. I've waited, and I think you're ready."

"Ready?"

"To dance with me."

His response shocked her. His assurance and arrogance pinched at her pride. A year ago, she had just begun to dance socially. She hadn't found her style then, hadn't known who she was when she danced, or even what she enjoyed. A lot had changed in twelve months.

"Am I?"

"I don't repeat myself. You're a sought-after dancer now. Steady on your feet. It's a powerful aphrodisiac. Men line up to ask you to dance, and yet you are just at the beginning. I can take you further. Make you better. I think you're ready."

"I thought you never repeated yourself."

His mouth curved; his expression softened. "So it would seem."

"How did you know my name?"

"I know a lot about you, Amira."

"Who are you?"

"I'm Batman."

She laughed even as she shook her head. "I may be younger than you, but I know when someone is evading questions."

"Do you? And how much older do you think I am?"

Though he kept himself trim and well-muscled, his face wasn't that of a twenty or thirty-year-old. But with men it could be hard to tell. She had a slew of gay friends to attest to that.

"I'm forty."

"I thought as much but didn't want to dent your ego."

"Men can be as vain as women. But neither of us care for that I think…My name is Zane."

"Zane. 'Gift from God.' It suits you."

He ignored her flippant response. "And forty? Does that suit you?" Even though he teased, his eyes were serious.

"I don't care for age. You can be old at twenty, or as young as Edward in his seventies. Numbers are deceptive."

"Numbers. What would you say if I asked for yours?"

"I'd say we have to dance first."

"Agreed. Dance with me." Satisfied, he closed his eyes, drawing her towards him. "I warn you now, I'm a stubborn man, used to getting my own way."

"Funny that, I was just about to say the same thing."

"A woman who knows her own mind. Very sexy, Amira."

He brushed his hand languorously from the small of her

back upwards, settling against her spine. Anticipation and desire created a new connection between them now.

She settled once more against his chest, opening her body to him. To whatever came next.

THAT NIGHT HER NEED WAS HOTTER THAN BEFORE.

Dancing with Zane had driven her to a point of unbearable arousal. She was giddy, all but floating home after their evening together. The lesson provided them an opportunity to connect, to explore one another's bodies. It was the most exquisite torture she had ever known. To be close to him, to touch him—finally—after all these months had exceeded her expectations. The minute she arrived home, she had raced upstairs to her room and slipped down her panties, letting them pool against her ankles.

She shivered at the cold night, brushing her hand down her thighs, yearning for contact. Her clit was sensitive after a night of foreplay. She alternated between quick pats and circular strokes, wanting to come fast and hard. Then do it all over again.

Her fingers, sticky and slick, trailed along her bare skin. Goosebumps followed in eager pursuit.

Lifting her skirt, desperate for sensations, Amira straddled the corner of her mattress, rubbing back and forth over the edge, driving her with each thrust wilder and wilder. Every time her hips rocketed back and forth, she thought of him.

Zane.

His chest, broad and heavy, pinning her to the mattress.

Those hands, skilled and soft tracing patterns on her naked body.

She ripped off her tank and freeing her breasts from her bra, she pinched her nipples, hard. Licking her fingers, Amira circled one straining tip and moved to the other, each time picturing Zane at her breasts, suckling, licking, rubbing his jaw against her until she begged for more.

She toyed with herself; the rough material of the blanket was just abrasive enough to provide the right amount of friction. But still she craved more. More heat. More contact.

More of *him*.

Amira knew it would be him. Had known it the moment they had touched. They were building towards something, her body sensed it.

Rough and shaking with her arousal, she increased the pace. She arched over the bed, breasts brushing against the blanket, the tug and pull of her orgasm beckoning like a seductive lover. Her clit was swollen, throbbing. She thrust against the bed, imagining his cock pounding into her from behind. She could still smell his aftershave lingering on her skin. It didn't take much for her to lose control.

With Zane's name on her tongue, she let go. Her orgasm rushed through her, a powerful force, consuming her body until she couldn't breathe.

Amira lay spread eagled against the cool cover, chest heaving. While her body slowly recovered, her mind was already racing. A reel of film played behind her closed eyes. Her body stirred.

She was already anticipating the next time.

CHAPTER THREE

AMIRA SENSED THE SHIFT IN THE AIR WHEN SHE CAME home from work that evening. It was an invisible rippling along her skin. A sense that tonight would be different. Not one to disregard her gut instinct, she showered with care, taking time with her appearance. She left her auburn hair unbound, letting it flow to her shoulder in loose waves.

Zane would be there, as he was every Thursday night. Since the lesson two months ago, they had developed an unspoken agreement. Every week they would attend Gus' *milonga* to dance. And every week she yearned for more.

Whilst their friendship was new, their conversations were rarely superficial. Even still, there was so much about him she had yet to learn. It fascinated her that a man as well-traveled and experienced as Zane hadn't wanted to settle down. To commit to one person.

His reasoning was vague, a strategy he used to dodge any personal questions. He was an individual very much in control. A man used to getting his way.

And she was addicted.

Amira liked who she was when they were together; open, candid, revealing parts of herself she never would with a stranger. But she wanted to dig a little further, to understand why she was drawn to him. In order to do that she needed to get to know the man behind the expensive suits.

Could he know of how often she fantasized about him? How often she came thinking about him inside her?

She thought he might have an inkling. And that suited her just fine.

Amira entered the *milonga* that evening, nerves in disarray. Feeling bold, she had worn her favorite silk dress. It was a daring design that showcased every inch of her body, hugging her ass and clinging to her curves; she was on display for those who dared to look.

But she cared only for one man's response. And when she stepped further into the hall, she was aware of it. That spark. And just as suddenly, her shoulders loosened, her muscles relaxed. She didn't regret her choice of outfit for a second.

She was attuned to Zane's presence. Like a pulse, she could sense him, strong and steady, just beneath the surface. She spotted him across the dance floor, sitting at the DJ table. Immaculate in yet another dark suit, he stared back at her, no doubt registering her shock. She was rooted to the ground. He never once mentioned he DJ'd tango music. But there he was, set up at the table, relaxed, in command, as if this was his regular gig.

Amira wandered to a group of dancers milling about at the edge of the floor. The lesson had ended for the evening, and a steady stream of people filled the hall. She took her time socializing, pleased when a few of the dancers complimented her on her dress, asking about her designs. Even though their conversation was engaging, the buzzing beneath her skin distracted her.

Yes, something was different tonight. She couldn't describe it, but she sensed it. With every nerve in her body, something was building.

She was about to excuse herself when one of the dancers moved closer, asking if he could claim the first *tanda*.

"She's spoken for."

Amira turned. Zane stood behind her and briefly rested his hand on her back, claiming the first dance. One reserved for lovers or friends.

He raised one dark eyebrow, a question of her acceptance.

"I am. But the second *tanda* is free."

The dancer nodded at her, then turned to Zane.

"DJ-ing on your own tonight?"

"As you see."

"It's all the rage nowadays to co-DJ. Not as much work. Happening a lot in Europe at the moment. I was just in Prague last month when a few of the top dancers did a few of the weekday *milongas* like that."

"I don't like to share." Zane stared at her now, his fingers trailing down her spine. The direct contact on her over-heated skin was a delicious torture.

She acknowledged his message with a raised eyebrow even as her body trembled. Her pulse danced to an odd rhythm. The rest of the conversation was lost on her. She was captivated by his lingering touch, by her desire for more. It seemed like an age before the music for the first *tanda* came on.

"I didn't know you DJ'd," Amira murmured when he led her to the floor.

"I appreciate the simple luxuries in life. Music is one of

them, especially tango. All those layers—the piano fighting with the violin, the *bandoneon* mediating between the two… it's captivating. I make it my personal creed to always invest in things that are pleasurable. Tell me, what do you do to relieve stress, Amira? When you're all alone at night?"

"Wouldn't you like to know?" she whispered.

"I would. I never ask unless I'm prepared for the answer."

The invitation hung in the air.

Zane opened his arms, and she stepped forward, accepting his lead. He was an exceptional dancer, a man in command of his body. He used the area around him not to showcase flashy moves, but to change direction, playing with technique, time and space. Because of it, her own dancing had improved. Alé and Tilda had even commented on it at her weekly lesson.

Zane's broad, solid body pressed against her breasts, promising another breathless dance. A *vals*. Romantic, grand, the epitome of elegance. Yet the conversation he had initiated was the exact opposite. She had never spoken about what turned her on. Never shared that with anyone.

For so long she was embarrassed by her sexuality. Sure that she was wanton for dreaming of sex, dirty for seeking out erotica. That sense of shame didn't exist when she was with him. It was liberating.

Whilst talking during dancing was generally frowned upon, the dialogue between them was murmured, low and for their ears only.

"Do you dream of this, I wonder?"

"Of tango?"

"Being held. Touched. Caressed." He slid a foot in between her own, shifting her axis, forcing her to slide her leg up and over his as they changed direction. His dark eyes captivated her, and she circled around him, slowly, never breaking contact.

"I dream of a lot of things."

"Come, Amira. Now's not the time to be shy. Tell me."

What dare she tell him? What would she reveal?

"What about sex?"

The thrill of his words rippled along her skin, calling for a response. Her breathing faltered, but her back remained upright, her body engaged.

"Doesn't everyone dream about it?" She didn't understand her sudden reticence. She craved this. On every level.

"I find dreaming about it second to the act of doing." The rumble of his voice next to her ear shook her resolve. He enticed her, teasing a part of her she believed to be taboo for so long.

"Yes…dreams are like foreplay; they only make me more aroused."

His hand tightened around her own. "What arouses you? Specifically?"

"Dancing. The weight of a man's chest against my breasts. The smell of his sweat and cologne. The pressure of his hand around my waist."

"Like this?" His voice was low.

"Yes."

His breathing had changed. It was imperceptible to those couples swirling around them, but not so to her. She wanted to excite him, to rip off the layers between them until he was naked and exposed.

What made him angry? Jealous? Stimulated?

Every interaction they shared, she learned a little bit more.

Despite their differences, they both understood what the other had to offer.

When the dance ended, he held her close. His heart raced against her chest, their breathing labored.

"Amira."

She could dance a thousand dances with a thousand men and never feel a whisper of what she shared with Zane. He spoke her name like a man tortured. She wanted to hear it again. Knew she would hear it when she awoke, wet and unfulfilled after another night alone.

But she didn't want to go home tonight. There was no color, no life in those traditional walls.

Reluctantly, they broke apart. After guiding her back to her table, Zane returned to his at the front of the room. She watched him DJ, talking to a steady stream of dancers but always returning his focus to the playlist. He worked intensely.

She couldn't recall who she had partnered with that evening, or how many times she was on the floor. Her mind, her body was with Zane. When she danced, he watched. Silent. Still. But with a careful consideration, the truth of which remained hidden.

That night, he altered their routine. Foolishly, Amira waited until the last *tanda*, hopeful he would ask her to dance again, only to find herself disappointed.

His restraint was confusing. Maddening. Her emotions ranged from shame to annoyance. Beneath it all was a stark realization that she was powerless. Traditional tango etiquette meant she would have to wait for him to ask her to dance. She had no control over the situation. Over him. She was not his lover, his girlfriend, not even a dear friend.

Caught in her own thoughts, she accepted Gus' request for

help to dress down the hall at the end of the evening. She welcomed the distraction, anything that would delay the return trip home.

Leaving the tablecloths behind the stage, Amira kept her head low, melancholy cradling her in its sleepy embrace. Her foot was barely on the first step when Zane approached, lifting her at the waist and lowering her to the ground. Her body slid against his, a tantalizing trail of lust following down, down, until it hovered at her belly button. Then lower still. The current shocked her back to life.

"Leaving so soon?"

"It's late. There's nowhere to go but home."

"I disagree."

Her stomach jittered.

"Don't play games with me, Zane."

"This isn't a game." He gripped her hips, studying her response.

A loud crash startled them both. At the far end of the hall, Gus cursed at the overturned chairs.

"Walk with me."

"Where?"

Zane held out his hand. It was a moment's hesitation. Annoyance still held her close, stroking her temper like a jilted lover.

"Outside. Where we can speak in private."

They slipped out into the cool evening air. The streets were quiet as midnight approached. All the sane people were already in bed, where she should be.

They walked in silence until Zane stopped at a sleek black vehicle. She was taken by the Art Deco inspired design, never having seen anything like it before. It was modern yet classic. Just like its owner.

Zane signaled to a man in an unmarked car parked behind it. The man nodded, driving away.

"Who was that?"

"Security."

"You have a babysitter for your car?"

He shook his head. "This isn't just any car."

Amira raised her eyebrows, not bothering to hide her disbelief. Even though it looked pricey, she was unfamiliar with luxury cars. If it cost more than a deposit for a house, it was too expensive.

"This is a Maybach Exelero."

"So?"

"Never mind."

"Wait. How much are we talking about here, for you to have a driver babysit a vehicle?"

Two men hovered a few meters away. Zane nodded for them to approach, and one bounded forward, phone poised to take pictures.

"For pity's sake." She stepped back, waiting until the two college students finished peppering Zane with questions. Their excited voices trailed from down the end of the street.

"More than some people's houses."

She didn't care that she probably looked like a fish out of water. "Like how many houses?"

"Enough to warrant a driver. Look, Amira, I'm not playing games with you."

A little of his façade seemed to slip away. His frustration made him real. Appealing. Less the rich acquaintance who kept himself at a distance.

"You could've fooled me." She studied the asphalt.

"You're upset."

"I have to go home."

"Amira." Zane tilted her chin. "I know when a woman is displeased. Tell me, what troubles you?"

"Right now, the excessively wealthy businessman who won't let me go home."

"And?"

"You ignored me tonight, Zane. I don't know why, but I thought…"

She was mortified to hear her voice crack. Gathering her emotions close, she breathed in, then cursed when all she could smell was *him*. She was tired. Emotional. She would not cry over the fact that he didn't dance with her, that he was turning her inside out.

"You thought correct. I apologize for the slight. But I couldn't dance with you tonight. Not after that first *tanda*. I couldn't trust myself to have you close, to touch you. Patience is not my strong suit. When I know what I want, I want it yesterday."

"And? What is it that you want, Zane?"

He stepped closer, his body radiating warmth. "I thought I made that clear tonight."

Amira gesticulated, annoyance still snapping at her heels. "No, Zane. With you, nothing is clear."

Firm hands gripped her waist. "Let me rectify that then."

She was burning. That was her first thought before everything else melted away.

He devoured her, the kiss possessive, heated. Every point of contact was like she was being incinerated. He clutched her dress, gathering her close.

She didn't care that her body betrayed her. Breasts heavy, chest heaving, she met his arousal with her own.

He spoke to her clearly now; the kiss communicated what remained unsaid.

Her body answered. Nipples straining against her dress, her back arched and curved. She threaded her hands in his hair and tugged, reveling in the thick, dark waves. And still she craved satisfaction.

"Amira…" His mouth travelled across her cheek, beneath her ear, distracting her. "Come home with me. Let me finish this. Properly."

There was no hesitation. But she stopped in spite of herself, wanting to see his face. "If I go home with you—"

"I will fuck you from now until dawn."

The words thrilled her, binding her body to his. "Take me home, Zane."

His grin, arresting and almost boyish, seized her. She didn't know a damn thing about this man, not really. Yet she knew she would have him.

Through her confidence, a tiny fissure emerged.

Once he realized the truth, would he have her too?

CHAPTER FOUR

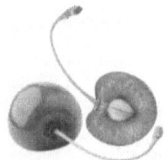

THE DRIVE TO ZANE'S HOUSE HAD NOT BEEN STRAINED despite the expectation that throbbed heavy around them. With every mile, a slick, slippery anticipation slithered over and around her resolve until her nerves were in disarray.

Sensing it, Zane placed a hand on hers and distracted her with conversation.

"You have to understand, all of this is only dear to me because of where I began."

Amira shifted to face him; curiosity piqued. "You mean you weren't born into all this?" She gestured out the window to the opulent houses sitting on display as he drove through one of Melbourne's most exclusive suburbs.

"Don't mistake me, I love nothing more than enjoying the lifestyle that money affords—"

"Tailored suits?" She caught the lapel of his jacket between her thumb and forefinger, stroking the fine material. Made to fit his body, his style. It spoke of a man who was confident, charming, and compelling at all levels. But Amira was beginning to understand what that actually meant.

He caught her fingers in his hand, kissing the tips before letting go. "Yes, fine clothes are essential. Once you know the feeling of silk against your skin, it's hard to settle for anything less. Something which I'm sure you would appreciate."

She settled back against the warm leather seat, the buzzing in her stomach returning. "Yes, that comes with the job description. I'm surrounded by fine material all day long." But being able to afford to wear it every single day was something else. "This car…how expensive is it anyway?"

He glanced over, smile hovering at his lips. "Does it matter?"

"Not one bit. But I'm a curious cat."

"You know what they say about cats…"

"That they get the cream?"

He laughed. "Very well. This cost just over eleven million."

Amira stared. The words filtered through her shock. "*Eleven* million? As in, dollars?"

"I don't trade in Monopoly money."

She laughed, incredulous. "Well. Wow. I can't say I've ever met anyone with that kind of spare change."

"I wouldn't say eleven million is spare change. But I'm willing to pay for my comfort. And I make sure those who tend to those comforts be compensated. My employees are paid well. They're loyal."

"You have staff? Like servants?"

"I have employees. Some who tend to my home, others who tend to my business. Both are vital to maintaining my lifestyle. Even though I have domestic help, they are all discreet. My privacy is important to me which means it is important to them. Anything you want, you shall have tonight."

Tonight. For the first time in her life, she would know what it was to be touched intimately. Sex. Another connection of sorts. She was under no illusions. Zane made her no promises. Had he done otherwise, she may not have been able to carry through with it.

The car began to slow down, and Amira's mouth gaped open. They stopped in front of a set of high gates, complete with security cameras and a guard.

"You live *here*?"

"Don't look so shocked."

"Just how successful is that business of yours?"

Zane laughed. "Business*es*. And in short, very. I've sacrificed a lot to get to this place, but I've come to appreciate where I'm at." He gestured beyond the imposing gates to the house on the hill. "This has come through a lot of hard work and some luck. But I've wanted this lifestyle for a long time. Now that I have it, I want to enjoy it."

"And you always get what you want."

"Eventually. And sometimes not at all. But I have fine tastes, Amira." His fingertip ran down her cheek as the gates swung open. He nodded to the guard as they drove by. "But then you already knew that."

"I'm surprised you don't have a driver."

Zane shrugged. "I do. For business, it's common sense. That time in the morning where I can work from the car makes me money. But never for nights of leisure. When I'm not working, I like to enjoy what I own. When they build cars so much like toys it's hard for me to resist." He winked, and it dawned on her then that she wanted more of him, of the playful, open man beneath the smooth exterior.

"I'd say most men would be in that category. My brothers for one."

"I don't blame them. When I was a little boy, I was given a luxury Ferrari. Don't look like that, it was one of those plastic toy cars."

"Like those Matchbox cars? My brothers guarded them like precious jewels."

"Yes. Except I was given mine by a rich boy I knew. I'll never forget that moment. The way he handed it over to me one day before my mother finished her shift, very casually mind you, as if he were handing over a rock, or some sticks. It was the first real gift I had ever known."

"Zane—"

"Let me explain. Ever since then, I had a burning inside me. You see, to that boy, that toy was worthless. He had five just like it, and a dozen more that were shinier, without all the nicks and scratches. But to me, it was the most priceless thing in the world. And I told myself that one day I would be rich like that little boy. And I would own the grandest, most expensive car. Not because it was given to me, but because I worked hard to buy it."

"That's an impressive story."

"It's the truth. I grew up poorer than dirt, and I'm not ashamed of that. But because of it, I appreciate what money can buy."

"Freedom."

"Exactly. To choose the kind of life you want to live. It affords you power so you never have to be caught in someone else's web."

He drove slowly up the winding path.

"So do you still have that toy car?"

Zane looked at her, as if weighing his words. He drummed his fingers on the steering wheel. "No. I…it's lost."

"Did you ever see the boy again?" She studied his face, wondering at the truth.

"That's a story for another day."

Before she could ask more questions, the house came into view. More like an estate than a home, but nonetheless architecturally arresting. The driveway was lit with small lights, guiding their way along the curved path to the sprawling mansion that sat at the pinnacle of the hill. To the left was a series of garages, to the right a circular gazebo.

A man opened the heavy double doors, nodding at her and smiling at Zane.

When they walked through the entrance, they were greeted by another man. Impeccably dressed and softly spoken.

"Champagne and refreshments in your suite, Mr. Zane."

"Thank you, Ahmed. I'll not require anything further."

Amira gazed in open admiration. Doors—now closed—flanked either side of the grand staircase. He held her hand, drawing her up two flights of stairs. They walked down more hallways, passing more rooms. What could a single man want with such a palace? The house was big enough for ten families, let alone one man.

They reached Zane's private rooms at the end of the hall.

"You live in this mansion alone?"

"I'm never alone."

"It's massive."

"And functional. But I wouldn't be paying my staff well if it weren't."

Zane opened double doors on the second floor. Opulent

was a word she clearly knew not of, not at this level. Whilst she could decipher between one superior cut of fabric from another, wealth like this surpassed anything she had experienced.

Everything in his sitting room, as he called it, was made for comfort: big, over-sized couches, plush, thick rugs. A massive fireplace, already lit, burned bright. Parallel to it, in the middle of the room, sat a rectangular table set with champagne, glasses and an assortment of sweet treats.

A veritable Eden. Summer fruits in the dead of winter. Pastries glazed and golden. And chocolate truffles piled high. A gift from God, indeed.

Zane gestured for her to sit, and he poured them a glass each.

Amira sipped, taking small bites of the food he placed before her. It kept her hands occupied and her mind focused. She savored the dark chocolate as it melted on her tongue. It was like nothing she had ever tasted.

The champagne should have taken the edge off. It should have eradicated her fears. Instead, it heightened the tension. Every doubt about her virgin status bubbled to the surface. What would he think of her?

Books and movies, not to mention her vivid imagination, only went so far. The truth was she could imagine what it would be like to suck a man's cock, but actually doing it was another matter entirely. Would she be any good? Would he?

Now was not the time to think about her sheltered life. Definitely not the time to worry about her parents' opinions. Despite their thinking, she was an adult, capable of making her own decisions. Her own mistakes. She would indulge in this one night of fantasy and then return to her conservative existence in the morning.

Amira cast a quick glance at the calm man seated across from her. He had taken off his jacket, his white shirt was unbuttoned, the sleeves rolled up. No, he wasn't a mistake. This wasn't some hasty decision or an error in judgment. It was something she wanted for a very long time. Now she would have it. Him.

The fire danced over his skin. He watched her, closely.

"Just to be sure, you want this, yes? Tonight…Sex."

"I wouldn't be here if I didn't."

"I know this. But I also know a mind can change. And I want a willing partner."

"You'll find me more than willing. Yes, Zane, I want this."

His head moved a fraction, accepting her response. He placed a raspberry in his mouth, chewing slowly. It made no sense why that turned her on.

"What pleases you, Amira?"

Sipping at her champagne, she sifted through the images that called to her. Above all else, she wanted to taste him, feel him in her mouth, to give pleasure. She told him so and had the very real satisfaction of seeing his hands grip the sides of the chair.

She set aside her champagne glass.

Zane sat forward, but she placed a firm hand on his chest.

"Let me."

He relaxed back into the cushion; eyes locked on hers.

"I thought I was the impatient one."

Slowly, with a confidence drawn from deep within her, she peeled back the buttons of his shirt, marveling at the bands of taut skin beneath her hands. He was warm, firm and utterly male. Her tongue circled one peck, then the other.

"Amira." His reaction spurred her on. She trailed kisses down his chest now, taking her time until she reached the belt at his waist. She marked a line across his waistband. She wanted to make him lose control.

The bulge in his pants jerked.

Amira bit her lip. With slightly shaking hands, she unzipped his pants, freeing him. She marveled at the thick, firm length that jutted before her.

Fears about her experience dissipated. Only her longing remained. She trailed a hand down his shaft, noting the veins that bulged, the heavy sacs at the base. He stiffened when she took one in her mouth, sucking. She did it again and heard his breath catch.

"Take off your dress."

Smiling, Amira shook her head.

"Amira. I want to see you naked."

Feeling confident, she drew down one strap, peeling away her bra, freeing one heavy breast.

Immediately his hand shot out, cupping her, fingers working over her nipple until she threw her head back. She gripped his cock, pumping her hand up and down. Her heart raced, her own desire winding around her, tighter and tighter. She shifted, panties suddenly too restrictive.

"Is this what you like?"

Zane groaned. He placed his hand around hers and increased the pressure. She continued until he started grinding his hips.

"Amira. If you don't stop, I'm going to come."

She lowered her head, eyes pinned to his, licking the

pearly white beads that gathered at the tip. He tasted salty, of sweat and sex. The heavy musk surrounded her, tantalizing, and forbidden. Lowering her head, she took him deep, enjoying the hard length at the back of her throat. She breathed him in, growing damp.

Zane titled his head back, eyes shut tight. With each motion, she pictured his cock thrusting inside of her. She was aroused by his reaction and thrilled to take him like this, to touch him so intimately.

He bunched his hands in her hair, guiding her head, setting the pace. She relaxed, breathing through her nose as he pumped.

"Can I come inside your mouth?"

She murmured an assent and continued sucking until he groaned, then stilled. A second later, hot, warm beads of cum filled her mouth. She swallowed, surprised at the volume and the salty-sweet tang. She wiped at her lip, her face hot, body on fire.

Zane lifted her up on his lap, holding her against his chest. His breathing evened out and he dipped her back, placing gentle kisses on her mouth.

She drew back, assessing his face, looking for answers. He seemed sated, content. She wanted to ask but couldn't find the words.

"I'm going to enjoy driving you wild. Consider it payback for what you just did." His finger traced the shell of her ear, stroking along her jaw.

Amira smiled, enjoying the banter. "Oh, I can be bad, Zane. A very bad little girl."

An eyebrow quirked. "Bad enough to be spanked?"

His hand trailed up her thigh, over her stockings to her

exposed breast. Expression hot, he flicked her nipple, tracing the peak with the pad of his thumb. Bolts of electricity shocked her system. His mouth swallowed her sigh, while his hand drove her wild.

"Yes."

In one fluid motion, he flipped her over. The breath rushed from her lungs. Her arms hung over the edge of the couch, and she braced herself on her elbows, straining her head to watch.

Steady hands guided her silk dress up over her legs, bunching it at her hips. He tugged down the scrap of cotton, exposing her ass. When the tip of his finger stroked the line between her cheeks, she shivered.

The first slap had her back arching in surprise.

"Is this how bad you've been?"

Amira shook her head. "I've been much, much worse."

The second smack stung. She gasped, surprised at her reaction. The pain was fleeting, but it heightened her desire. She urged him on, waiting with bated breath for his hand to make contact. She squirmed; with every smack she grew desperate for him to touch her, to take her.

She had never been more turned on in her life. There was a world of sin out there and she was eager to sample it all.

"The sound you're making is driving me fucking wild. Keep that up and I'll have to punish you."

"I have a better idea." Amira slowly turned in his arms, sore and nowhere near satisfied. That was about to change.

"Liked that, did you?" He peeled off her panties, tossing it aside.

"What gave me away?"

Zane nudged her knees apart, then trailed a finger over her

stockings until it rested at the thatch of curls between her thighs. He lifted his hand, fingers glistening and wet.

"Does this answer your question?"

Amira guided his hand back to her clit. The pressure of his fingers was a delicious torture. She spread her legs wider, eager for him to touch her where no one else ever did. She was at his mercy, every stroke a step closer to release.

The build-up was slow. His smile, wicked. He toyed with her, advancing and retreating, until she gripped his arm. She closed her eyes and could only imagine what she looked like, spread before him as he pleasured her. Next time they would use a mirror. She wanted to see him touch her this way. To watch as she lay exposed and vulnerable. Her clit began to pulse and she nearly sobbed with relief.

Dipping his dark head, he sucked her nipple.

"Please, Zane."

"Please, what?"

Her eyes flashed open. She sensed he was about to retreat, and she clutched at his hand.

"Don't you fucking dare."

"Tell me, do you want me to stop?"

"Like hell."

"Or is this better?" He continued now, giving her what she craved. "Is this the spot, my sweet Amira? Is this what you're begging me to do?"

"Make me come, Zane. Touch me."

With a few deft strokes, he sent her hurtling over the edge. She writhed beneath his expert touch, hips jerking as her orgasm pounded through her. She peaked and shattered over and over until she lay spent, sprawled across his lap. She was floating, drifting, at peace. Zane gathered her close, placing a kiss on her nose.

"*That* was all my pleasure."

Amira laughed, body limp.

"That sound suits you."

"What?"

"Joy. Your laugh, it's like someone turned on a light. It fills the room."

She hugged the compliment to her chest.

"Just like pleasure. That suits you, too. A woman who looks the way you do, who dances like you, is one who was meant for hours of this." Zane picked up a raspberry. Biting one half he guided the other to her mouth, watching as she bit into it. Each time he fed her, her desire grew. As did his, the hard length rising beneath her bottom.

She reached over to the table, picking up the pot of melted chocolate. Dipping her index finger in the dark liquid, she watched as he sucked it clean. Taking the small glass container from her hand, Zane tilted it until the warm chocolate hit her nipple. He traced the path with his tongue, grazing his teeth along the heavy curve of her breast in quick bites. He licked her breast until she shuddered.

"Time to move to somewhere with a little more room. If you're still keen?"

Amira stood, stretching out her hand. "Lead the way."

He guided her to his bedroom, placing small, sweet kisses up her neck, whispering in that deep, drugging voice, of all the ways he would touch her. Take her. It was as if he had been in her dreams. He had picked every fantasy and fed it back to her with greater clarity, depth, emotion.

Creams and greys blurred around her, but all she could see

was him. A large bed lay in the center of the room, dark blue and white. Everything in the room was masculine, classy. A reflection of the man before her.

Zane touched and tasted, driving her wild, until they landed on the covers.

He stood back, shedding the rest of his clothes but stilled her hand when she tried to do the same.

He wrapped his fingers under the sheer elastic at the top of her thighs, drawing back the stockings down her past her knees, then off her feet. First one leg, then the other, he feasted like a man starved.

Her pulse kicked.

He took his sweet time, grinning at her response. "Your reaction to me is intoxicating. Every moan makes me want to fuck you. To come inside you. To drive you insane."

"Then do it, Zane. Fuck me."

His eyes narrowed. "Not yet. I want to taste you first."

He pulled her to the edge of the bed. She was naked and spread out on the covers, eager for his touch.

The first lick sent her hips flying. It was an ecstasy that far exceeded her expectations. He gripped her hips, tongue rubbing her clit. Zane alternated between slow swirls and fast strokes, until his tongue burrowed inside her. The pressure, the resistance, set her heart racing.

"Relax, Amira. Let me drive you wild."

And he did.

He varied the speed, the pace, lapping at her until she was dripping and straining against his mouth. Just like his dancing, he was adept at changing direction, at responding to her rhythm, leading her until she lost all thought, all control. His fingers toyed with her now. One, then two. The pinch became a sting. It burned and branded her to him. Her first.

Amira dragged him up to her, over her. She tasted herself on his lips, sweet, so incredibly sweet.

"More, Zane. I want you inside me."

When he covered himself with the thin sheath, she stilled.

He took her hips and tilted them slightly. Kissing her, he teased, his cock jutting at her clit, rubbing at her pussy. In one motion he thrust into her.

Amira gasped at the pain. Sharp shooting arrows dulled her pleasure. Every inch of her body froze as she bared down against the intrusion.

"You're so tight," he gasped, mouth at her neck.

Zane reared back. "Amira? What's wrong?"

She shook her head. "Keep going."

He did the opposite. "I'm hurting you."

"No…" she looked at the ceiling. "You're…big. Or I'm… small…" She couldn't say it. Didn't want to say it, to break the spell.

He guided her face to his. "How to damn with faint praise. But you're not enjoying this, I can see it." In one fluid move, he flipped them over, reversing roles. "You set the pace." He winked, inching back up to the headboard. He lay there, arms crossed behind his head, biceps bulging. "Take me at your leisure, sweet Amira. We have all night."

Stalking up the bed with newfound confidence, she brushed her body up the length of his thick calves, past his jutting cock until her breasts hovered at his mouth. She watched him suck her nipples, and smiled when those hands shifted, gripping her ass.

Amira moved down, straddling him.

Lowering herself on the tip of his cock, she breathed out. The familiar pinch and burn drilled through her. The resistance clear. Frustration made her movements stilted. Self-conscious.

Was she too small? He too big? She tried to relax her muscles around him, afraid she might never get past the initial barrier. She wasn't doing it right.

Irrational fears echoed inside her mind. Afraid she would be a virgin all her life, she lowered herself down further, desperate for him to fit.

"Relax. We have all night." He reached in the drawer by the bedside table and spread the lubricant on his cock.

She straddled him again, gasping when his fingers toyed with her nipples. Sensations swamped her taut body. She rubbed at her clit, hovering over him, sliding down by degrees, the burning at her core threatening to overwhelm her, to rob her of her desire.

On the precipice between pleasure and pain, Amira pressed on, feeling as if she would split in two. He held onto her waist, moaning. She continued until every inch of his cock was buried inside her. She shuddered at the new sensation. Leaning forward, she took the time to adjust around him.

"Easy, Amira. Nice and slow."

She kissed him now, soft, sweet kisses, claiming her arousal. He pulsed inside her, his body unmoving. A telltale dampness soaked through the strain. Relief accompanied it. And as her fears began to subside, so did the pain. She slid up and down his cock, mouth fused to his, hand working over her clit.

"Can I?"

She nodded, letting him thrust beneath her, setting the

pace. The pain danced around her, in step with her building orgasm. Every movement brought her closer to pleasure, every inch brought her closer to pain. She was bound to him in every way, eager for him to keep going.

Sobbing, she urged him faster, her own fingers flying. But he kept the same steady pace until she bowed above him. The rushing of her orgasm stole any pain she might have felt. It surrounded her, engulfing every thought, every doubt, until she shattered.

It wasn't long before Zane cursed, thrusting harder. Gripping her ass, he came, muscles straining, body hard as granite.

She slumped over him, limbs heavy, heart light.

In a wonderous haze, Amira eventually shifted above him. Then frowned. Her fingers were slick with sweat and tinged… with blood. The violence of it was smeared across her thighs. The bed. *Him.*

Her heart bounded against her chest. As if on a roller-coaster, she couldn't catch her breath.

"Amira?"

Zane glanced at her hand, the fingers stained red.

He looked up at her, understanding replacing his momentary confusion. "That only happens once."

His words shook her into action. She sprang back, body shivering.

Amira barely registered the tears on her face. Like some stupid cliché, she allowed him to hold, to soothe, as her quiet sobs punctuated the darkness. She was sore, empty, her body reminding her of what had just occurred. She closed her eyes against the sight.

She wanted the romance. To be swept away by her lust,

flying through her arousal. But the sharp stinging pain was evidence of what she had done.

She didn't regret it for a minute. She just hadn't expected *this*. The after. Or her reaction. Tiny goosebumps travelled across her arms and chest, like invisible reminders of who she was, and who she was with…

She had sex. With Zane. She was no longer a virgin; she would never die an old maid. But she hadn't expected the tidal wave of emotions and was embarrassed by the force of it. By his conciliatory reaction.

These feelings had no place in her fantasies. No place here between them.

Because he *was* her fantasy, or at least had been for so long. A man whose world was so far removed from her own, he had offered her a taste of it. Which is where it would stay.

Damn him. Damn her stupid mind. This was supposed to be light. Fun. Without any emotions or interfering thoughts. But she looked down at her fingers, the smudges marking her hands.

"Amira, talk to me. Are you okay?"

She nodded, unable to open her mouth. What would she say?

"I would have taken my time, if I had known." He tilted her chin to face him. "I'm not blaming you. I'm honored to be your first and hate to think I've hurt you. For that I'm sorry."

"I was afraid you would be able to tell or something." She sounded so childish, so naïve. She shifted, wanting to shake free of it.

"I should have figured it out, but I'm on the larger side of normal." He raised his eyebrows, eyes shining. "If you know what I mean?"

Amira sniffed. "Objective too."

"I'm honest to a fault…"

He held her close, kissing her shoulder blade, the column of her throat. His thumbs, wide and smooth, drew circles on the sides of her body. Despite her pain, despite her mortification, her nipples hardened.

"It's a perfectly normal reaction. This is your first time. I'm your first."

She studied him now and saw the satisfied male pride. It didn't make her want to slap him. She had grown up with men knowing their worth. Or inflating it. In his eyes she saw respect.

"I'm honored you chose me."

"There you go repeating yourself, Zane."

The rumble in his chest warmed her own. "Only with you. I think I'm a little in shock too."

And she knew he understood. Her body, cold and jittery, warmed to his touch, his words.

Because he was right. She *did* choose him. Her body had chosen him long before her mind had made the decision. But thinking about something and experiencing it was not one and the same thing. His reaction to her eased the tumult and shame. It reminded her of why they were there, why she chose him.

He traced her lips, her nose, her jaw. "I have twin shower heads and heated bath towels waiting. Give yourself some time to relax. I'll pour more champagne, if you would like to stay for a drink?"

She shook her head. She didn't want space, didn't want to be alone. She wanted him. "Join me?"

The heat in his eyes was more than just sympathy.

Zane stood, lifting her to the bathroom, and placing her down in the shower as if she were a precious jewel. He washed away any traces of their sex, and her virginity. And inch by inch, her need bloomed until she directed the shower head down between her thighs. Her appetite had no limits.

"Show me, Amira. What do you do when you're alone? I want to watch."

She guided the spray between her legs.

His mouth nuzzled her breasts, teeth grazing her nipples, until she directed him lower. Spreading her legs apart, he feasted. Amira ignored the pulling tenderness and focused on the hands that shifted to her bottom, kneading her flesh while his tongue devoured her clit.

"Zane, take me."

She watched his dark head between her legs, the way he pumped his cock, jerking himself off. Their moans bounced off the shower walls, echoing across the tiles.

It wasn't long before they each found release, lingering in the warm spray. She enjoyed washing his body, allowing herself the luxury of touching him, of showering with a man.

She was sated, blissfully whole. Completely at ease.

They both knew a repeat performance wouldn't be in the cards. Not tonight. Maybe not ever.

Wrapped in a lush cream robe, Amira let him lead her to the sitting room. Back in front of the fire, she shared his seat. "One drink before I go?"

He inclined his head. His kiss was soft, lingering. "One drink."

WHEN THE SUN CAME UP TO GREET THEM THE NEXT morning, Amira didn't question what had happened.

No shame. No regrets.

She was smugly satisfied and utterly relaxed.

When Zane opened his eyes ten minutes later, she was struck by an odd sensation. It lingered between them when he drew her close, placing kisses along her chest. It hovered above them as he stroked her lazily, drawing out her need. It even curled up beside her when they lay spent in a sweaty heap.

It was only when Zane brought her breakfast on a silver platter that the thought manifested itself, ringing clear and true.

A sense that their story had only just begun.

SEX AND THE STAGE

SWEET, SEXY SCANDALOUS BOOK 2

A Sweet, Sexy, Scandalous Series

Sex
and the
STAGE
~ BOOK TWO ~

IDA BRADY

CHAPTER ONE

THEY WERE ABOUT TO HIT THE STAGE ON THE MOST important night of his career, but all Alé could think about was burying himself inside Tilda's hot, wet pussy.

He should have been focusing on the performance, the judges, hell, even the audience, but he had a raging hard-on that wouldn't fucking quit.

Madre de Dios. Did he never learn? Now was *not* the time for a quickie.

Not that it ever stopped him before.

Tonight would determine whether he would be crowned the *Mundial de Tango* World Championship winner. God knew he was no king. He had coveted the title for over a decade. The title that had been robbed from him all those years ago.

His back twinged. The phantom remembrance a distant echo of the man he used to be. His body was strong. His mind was healed. All because of the woman beside him. The woman who helped him realise what a *culo* he had been. Alé didn't know what he had done in a past life to deserve her, but he wouldn't be letting go of the best thing that happened to him. He'd be a fool to even try.

"Alé…I know that look."

"What?"

Dios. She was stunning. Her body was on display; the scraps of red lace showing off the curve of her breasts, the round swell of that ass. If he wasn't careful, he'd lose himself in her. It wouldn't be the first time. The fact that they were connected by law, that she was now his wife, was a greater turn-on than he ever would have imagined.

But he needed to remain focused. If they won the title it would create new opportunities for their business. For their dancing. But he was thinking too far ahead. They had to get through the first round of performances.

Or not.

The backstage area was filled with a flurry of activity. There was a humming of movement, the whispers and directives thrown around in between performances mingled with the music surrounding them.

Never in all his wildest dreams would he have thought he would be here. But a lot had happened in the past three years. Tilda was no longer scared of performing. Their dancing was the best it had ever been. Fluid. Powerful. Dynamic. Tilda was flawless, her confidence present in every *adorno*, every extension. It was a thrill to dance with her. But even knowing that, competing for something that he had worked so long and hard to achieve still left him on edge.

Alé knew the perfect solution to calming those nerves.

"Alé? Are you okay?"

"I have something important I want to discuss with you, Tilda."

"Now?"

"*Sí.*"

"But we'll be on soon. Can't it wait?"

He shook his head, holding her hips. "It's an *urgent* issue."

A line of concern formed between her pretty blue eyes. He tried not to smile. "It's about this *very* sexy dress you have on." He stroked the curve of her waist and found bare skin. Parts of the material were left out to make the costume sexier. It worked. Every man, woman and judge had watched Tilda walk through the change area. Other dancers commented on her outfit, the women with envy, the men with greedy appreciation.

All that golden blonde hair was tucked away, bundled up at the base of her neck in a neat coil. He loved seeing it loose, flowing down to her waist. Especially when she was naked.

"What about my dress? Is there a tear?" She glanced down, frantically searching.

Alé held her shoulders. "*Sí*, it's about the dress."

"*Where*? I don't have time to change into the back-up outfit Amira made."

Alé walked her slowly backwards, a smile sneaking through. He loved teasing her. Loved her reaction. *Dios*, he loved every little thing about her. "Trust me, I'd be the first to tell you if there was a tear. But your dress is just…" he sighed. "Too. Fucking. Sexy."

Tilda's shoulders slumped. She swatted his arm. "You rat! You had me worried for a minute."

"You should be worried. Because I intend to have you in that dress. Right here. Right now."

She rolled her eyes. "Very funny, Alejandro. Hey, where are we going?"

He sidestepped them both, leading her with a series of turns until they stopped behind swathes of heavy curtains. He found a smooth patch of the wall that wasn't filled with props and pressed her back against it.

Tilda's eyes were wide.

"Alé…"

He closed the space between them, grinding his hips against hers.

An incredulous look flittered across her face before she chided him. "Are you crazy?"

"Only for you."

Her embarrassed laugh raced up his spine. He never got tired of hearing that sound.

"That's corny even for you."

When he dipped his finger beneath the thin scrap between her thighs, she gasped. She was warm and giving. The silk grew damp with every stroke, encouraging him further. Her eyes grew distant, her body strained.

Alé ground his teeth together. He wanted to devour her whole.

"What if people see? We'll be disqualified!"

"Then we just have to be careful."

Tilda pulled him closer, gripping the lapels of his jacket. She whispered against his ear, lips brushing the sensitive curve. "Then hurry up and fuck me, husband. Before I come on your fingers."

"Keep talking like that, *wife*, and you won't be the only one to lose control."

He unzipped his trousers, loosening his belt. Freeing himself, he lifted one of Tilda's legs, the warmth of her bare thigh spurring him on. He could spend hours exploring her body. He would once this was all over.

The pre-cum gathered on the tip of his cock. He smeared it down his shaft. There was no time for lubrication, no time for slow and steady. He spat on his palm for good measure. Images of his wife sucking him off fired through his mind: those lips, painted a bold red, wrapped around his cock as he pumped into her. It made him even harder.

Alé groaned, entering her slowly, inch by glorious inch until he was buried deep. That sensation, the feeling of her pussy stretching around his cock, was the hottest thing he had ever known. He shuddered. Desire and expectation wound around him now, squeezing tight. That moment of surrender, when her body accepted him, warm and hot and willing, made him feel like a king.

Alé pulled back—almost all the way out—before thrusting in, a little harder this time. He set a rhythm, teasing them both. He wanted to rip away the material of her dress. To feast on those breasts but gripped her bare ass instead.

The curtain behind him shifted, and he froze.

Tilda's eyes grew round. She seized his arms shaking her head. A silent warning.

A man and a woman's voice floated behind them. A stream of words, heated and in Spanish, filtered through the curtain. They were arguing about their performance. He watched Tilda's face, a wicked idea forming.

Heart bouncing in his chest, he slowly pulled back and thrust into her. Alé ground his teeth together, afraid he would laugh and expose them both.

Her eyes, expressive and clear, spoke volumes. He grinned.

The combination of her tight pussy and the imminent

danger of being found fucking behind the curtain set his blood pumping. *Dios*, he was harder than granite. Hornier than a school kid. And more in love with his wife than ever before.

He thrust in and out, slowly at first, then with a reckless frenzy. Her sharp gasps spurred him on. When her head fell back against the wall behind her, he knew she was close. He loved nothing more than to give her this. To watch as she lost all thought, lost all control.

As the arguing couple's voices grew louder, he squeezed Tilda's butt and lifted her up off the ground. Pressing her against the wall, he used it as leverage, holding her in place while he pounded into her.

And then he felt the curtain shift behind them. A whisper of a breeze.

Before he could react, a third voice cut through the couple's argument, directing the pair to shut up or get out.

Gradually, the footsteps moved further away, only to be replaced by a voice calling for the dancers to begin last minute costume adjustments. It was time to line up.

He bit down on the sensitive curve of Tilda's neck. She moaned, chest heaving. She was close. Sweat gathered beneath his shirt; his arms and shoulders were burning. His cock was ready to explode.

"Come for me, Tilda."

And then he felt it. The delicious spasms as she clenched around him, milking his cock, driving him closer and closer to the edge. Watching her face, those full lips parted, those eyes lost in pleasure, was all he needed to take him over.

"Tilda," he ground out.

She blinked, her dazed expression slowly clearing.

"I'm gonna explode. I need to pull out." The tell-tale rush was building. He wouldn't be able to stop if he kept going.

A feline smile crossed her face. It was enough to burn through his restraint.

"Put me down."

He lowered her, slipping out, feeling the absence of her warm, wet pussy. Then he shuddered. Her mouth wrapped around his cock, working him, keeping that steady pace that drove him insane. And like that, he was lost. Those bold red lips, those pretty blue eyes. The contrast of her wicked innocence hit every point of desire.

He grabbed her shoulders, clenching his jaw. That second before coming, the pure rush of heat, the build-up and release, was better than anything he had ever known. Because of her.

Gasping, he came into her mouth and watched as she sucked him dry, swallowing every drop. *Dios*, he wanted to fuck her all over again.

When the rushing in his ears subsided, Alé helped her stand, his own arms aching.

Rearranging her dress, Tilda shook her head but smiled in satisfaction.

"You're a naughty little Argentine, Mr. Garcia."

"I thought you liked that about me."

"I love that about you…but I need a bathroom or we're going to be disqualified for *dishabille*."

"Talk French to me again."

She pecked him on the lips, laughing. "You're pushing it, lover boy." She peeked her head out from the far end of the curtain then walked as quickly as possible along the wall, head bent low, avoiding eye contact.

He didn't know why their act of forbidden sex made him

feel closer to her, but it did. Alé sent up a silent prayer of thanks. He would be forever grateful that she chose him.

Fixing his clothes, he counted to sixty then walked out from behind the curtain, following her.

The call for dancers rang out again.

It was time for the show to begin. They had a title to win.

CHAPTER TWO

"*MUSICA MAESTRO.*"

They had made it to round three and were dancing with the finest couples from all around the world. Carlos Di Sarli's *Esta Noche De Luna* came on. A sprightly, lively piece. Alé was energized. Having sex with Tilda not only decimated any nerves, it also reinvigorated him. His body was relaxed. His mind clear.

He settled into the piece ignoring the other dancers, the lights, the murmur of the audience; it may as well be just him and Tilda on the stage. When he danced with her it was like nobody else in the world existed. She surrounded him in every way: the pressure of her chest, the comforting weight of her hand, the smell of her perfume mixed with sex...he couldn't get enough. He would have her again before this night was over.

He positioned her into a *calesita*, moving around her so she turned like a ballerina in a music box. He stepped back, turning it into a *carpa*, a tent like positioning. It was then that he noticed her expression, the tense set of her shoulders, the way she clutched his hand.

Something was wrong.

Her dress was still in place, it was pretty much glued on, but something was off. Had her shoe strap come undone? A tell-tale foreboding clutched at his stomach. A familiar unease wound its way around them, seeking entry. But there was no room for a third in this embrace.

Madre de Dios. There was no room for any break in his concentration. And even though he knew this song as well as he did his wife's lithe body, he needed every part of his mind focused on her. On them. On this damned competition.

His mind whirred with possibilities; he could only hope his expression remained unfazed.

It wasn't show tango, but in the *Tango de Pista* division that they were competing, which meant improvised dancing and responding to the music they were given without any pre-planned choreography. It meant no distractions.

"Stay with me, *mi corazón*."

"Every step."

And then he saw it.

Saw *her*.

"*Puta madre*."

He should have expected it. Should have known that *she* would be here. He caught a glimpse of her, watching them off stage. The same cool smirk was plastered on that face from three years before.

But he was not the same man.

More importantly, this night wasn't about *her*. Or the past. Channeling his energy into the woman in his arms, he ignored the prickling sensation that pierced across his skin.

He focused on the rise and fall of Tilda's chest against his own. The soaring violins and yawning *bandoneon* called him to action. He displaced her feet, slicing his leg inside her bare thigh. She was warm, the remnants of sex still lingering on her body. He savored it and the memory of her wrapped around him as they danced.

Tilda executed a series of pretty *adornos*, showcasing the complexity in her repertoire and the flashy *Commes* on her feet. He stole a glance at her face: pure concentration and not an ounce of fear. His woman was not only beautiful, but she had a spine of steel too. It made him proud.

He stole another glance at his wife and the encouraging smile she threw his way. She was enjoying this. The woman who vowed never to dance on stage was caught in a joy he was not allowing himself to feel.

He was no good. They would never win. He was weak.

The past hovered around him, seeking entry.

He focused on his wife, on the life they had built. And just as suddenly, the fear dissipated. Tilda's courage was a balm on his wounds. The woman had endless faith in him. In them.

He would make her proud.

Before he could let his mind wander, the audience clapped. The song ended, giving them a chance to check in with one another before the next dance.

Ricardo Tanturi. *Ese Sos Vos*. Another jovial piece. Sharp violins. Trilling piano. A waterfall of sounds and beats peppered the way for Tanturi's rich, smooth voice. Its power and pace transfixed his mind, and Alé succumbed to it with relief.

It seemed like only seconds before the next song came on. Juan D'Arienzo. *El Simpatico*. The final piece in this round.

Quick, piercing violins contrasted to the movement of the piano, up and down the scale. He noticed the *ganchos* and *boleos*, the varied styles of nine other couples, showcasing the music in their own way. It reminded him of how far they had come, how much they had achieved.

Tilda's breath was close to his ear. The energy that surrounded them when they danced was a tangible force. The way he held her, he held no one else. The way she moved for him, she did with no one else.

Together they were unstoppable. It was the sex. The love. The powerful connection that made them so compelling.

Alé had danced with many over the years. And nothing, nobody, ever affected him the way Tilda did. Whether they won or not, he had fulfilled a dream. More importantly, he had done it with the woman he loved. The one he almost lost. He wouldn't ever make that mistake again.

But still the question remained: what the hell was *she* doing here?

"*Hola*, Alejandro."

"Camila." Alé stiffened when she leaned in to kiss him on the cheek.

"And you must be Tilda. I've heard so much about you."

"Watch it, Morales."

He had the satisfaction of seeing her jerk back as if scalded.

"Now, now, is that any way to speak to an old friend?" Her fake pout turned into a sly grin. "She *is* pretty, Alejandro. Much prettier up close."

"Can we help you with anything?" Tilda's expression was cool. Distant. "If not, we really have to prepare before the final piece."

"That's no way to speak to a guest judge."

"I beg your pardon?"

"Ignore her. Camila, I don't know what games you're playing, but we don't need to be a part of it."

Camila shook her head, smile growing. "You don't believe me?"

"I stopped believing you a long time ago."

He would not react. It only fuelled her sick agenda.

She shrugged, affecting boredom. "Suit yourselves."

"Camila, you're on in five." The stage coordinator called out to her before being distracted by a technical issue.

Tilda's gasp was low, but audible.

Alé gritted his teeth, refusing to let her have the satisfaction. Anger bubbled beneath his skin. Old memories, even older wounds split open, slicing at his resolve. His calm.

But like a speeding train, his temper once in motion, was difficult to stop. "How many favors did you have to suck or fuck to pull this one off, Camila?"

"Alé...don't."

Camila's wicked laugh was soft, dangerous.

"Oh, Alejandro. Always underestimating me."

"I thought I made myself clear three years ago. What the hell are you doing here?"

"Like I said. I'm a *guest* judge. And whilst I enjoyed watching you and your novice girlfriend play at dancing, I can't quite say I thought it was winner quality."

"You manipulative—"

Tilda's arms held him. He wanted to march that stupid bitch out of the competition and far away from his wife.

A judge. A guest judge. *Dios*. Would he ever be rid of this woman? Weren't the scars on his body reminder enough of his past? Of the pain she had caused? Why was she here, now?

Impotent rage coursed through him. "What is this, Camila?"

"I told you you'd be nothing without me. I meant it. Whenever you dance, I'll be there. Whenever you compete, you'll know I was a part of it."

"You need to leave us alone. Get some help."

The façade began to fade. "Help?" She shrieked, face contorting in derision, dark eyes flashing in disgust. It took her a few minutes to control herself, but in that time, Alé understood that she was trapped in that same place he was all those years ago. But unlike him, she chose to remain there. To feed that hatred, to let it blossom into whatever it was that sheltered her now.

Camila's face assumed a neutral expression, covering the ugly woman inside. She stepped closer, hissing. "He robbed me of my dreams. Of everything I worked so hard to achieve. And you speak to me of help? Stupid girl. I don't need anyone's help. I've learnt to help myself. But you'll learn that the hard way. So, here I am, guest judge after all these years."

He had heard the swirling rumors from the *Nuevo* vanguard, those who wanted to spice up the traditional form of the competition. Those who pushed for change to not only the way the competition was judged, but the style of tango that was considered legitimate. And if it was one thing he knew, it was the way his ex-girlfriend's mind worked.

He knew Camila, unfortunately for him. She was sly.

Calculated. *Mundial de Tango* was a traditional competition with rules and regulations that did not bend or break. Yet here she was. Her clout in Buenos Aires was stronger than he expected.

"You have to let this go. Alé and I have moved on. You need to do the same."

"You heard her. Piss off, Camila."

"A little backbone, Alejandro. Finally."

Camila was ushered closer to the stage. She shrugged, then slunk away, not before calling back over her shoulder. "Oh, and Tilda? Good luck."

They watched her take place on the stage with her dance partner. It took all of Alé's restraint not to shove her into the crowd. He gripped Tilda's hand, breathing in slowly, forcing the white-hot rage to subside.

Seconds later, the announcer called for silence.

"As a surprise to all audience members who wrote in, texted or tweeted, we have a special guest judge tonight. Ladies and gentlemen, it is with great pleasure that I present to you, Camila Morales, runner up of the 2006 *Mundial* and dancer in the television show *Dance to Win: All Stars* with Alberto Lopez. She's been watching the show backstage and will contribute to the overall scores of the judges. Her vote may be the one that tips the scales for one lucky couple. Please welcome Camila Morales and her partner, Alberto Lopez, as they dance to Juán D'arienzo's version of the classic, *La Cumparsita. Musica Maestro!*"

Tilda cupped his face. "Look at me. No, don't do that. Don't go back there. Alé, stay focused."

"I'm here. I am. *Dios,* I'm so fucking angry. I want to wring that bitch's neck."

"I know. So am I, but we can't let her get to us. She's done enough damage over the years. I won't allow her to do it to us again. To you."

He paced the small space. "I thought I made it clear to her three years ago."

"You can't control her. Getting angry isn't going to change anything. She's here. I don't know how it happened, but there's not much we can do right now. The formal judging is over, so let's just finish this competition on a strong note. I refuse to let that woman take this from us. I don't care how we place in this competition, Alé, but I do care about you."

"*Sí.*" He squeezed her shoulders, drawing her in. "I know this. But the thought of her somehow interfering. Again—"

"I get it. But we can figure it all out later. Now isn't the time to think about Camila Morales."

Alé rested his forehead against hers, then kissed the tip of her nose. "You're right. It isn't."

"I know I'm right. But you need to work off some of that mad."

"Have something in mind, do you?" He winked.

"Down boy. I meant to walk it off. *Alone.*" She nudged him toward the exit. "You don't need to watch Camila and Alberto dance. I'm sure you won't miss anything anyway. Get some fresh air, and I'll see you in five."

Even though he didn't want to leave her, he knew she was right. He needed to take all that anger and burn it before it engulfed them both.

CHAPTER THREE

AND JUST LIKE THAT IT WAS OVER. IT WAS THE END OF the competition. They had the final group choreographed routine before the winners were announced. The judges were already backstage tallying scores, determining dreams. One hardworking couple would take the prize.

He wanted it to be them more than he cared to admit.

Now that his head was clear, and the judging over, Alé allowed himself to relax. He was determined to enjoy the final dance. A dance that their friend, Isabella, had helped choreograph.

He would not think about Camila Morales or his future being determined by her whims. He would not allow bitterness to dictate his actions anymore. Even though it would hurt to lose, he would carry on. Build new dreams.

"You okay?" Tilda squeezed his hand, her warm body close, comforting, familiar. He could face anything with her beside him.

"*Si*. Let's show 'em how we do it, eh?"

The music filled the large auditorium. In a chorus line,

they all moved together as one. Twenty couples on the stage, in time to the music.

He was aware of everything: the stage, the couples, his wife. She danced with such confidence now it was hard to believe she was the shy bookstore owner who had stumbled into his studio all those years ago. But she had shown him what it meant to be a man. One who was no longer haunted. He was no longer broken.

This competition had been the final fuck you to his past. It had given him that final piece of closure. And damn, it felt good.

As the music reached its crescendo, Alé turned Tilda in his arms, preparing for the lift. Within a few steps she was up, high over his head. He held the position, and bending his knees slightly, sprang her up into the air. Tilda spun, once, twice, then landed with the grace of a cat in his arms. Her body arched, her leg extended.

They paused, holding the final pose. His chest heaved; his muscles strained.

Alé grinned, watching his wife as the thunderous applause rang through the auditorium.

His chance at the title, to win this competition, was finally over.

He never felt more alive.

Murmured words of encouragement filtered through the audience as the couples lined up on the stage. They waited like eager children to learn of their fate.

This was the moment. Years of training, injuries, hours spent honing their craft, it all lead to this.

After thanking the sponsors, the participants and the guests, the judges made the announcements.

Alé held his breath.

When another couple stepped forward claiming 5th place, his heart pounded.

The countdown began. It was a slow torture watching the lucky couples as they placed.

4th. 3rd.

When it got to 2nd, his mouth went dry. His hopes of winning suddenly seemed impossible. The stark truth hit home. They hadn't won. It was over.

He focused on Tilda's hand in his, holding tight. While his body buzzed, she was calm beside him. Then it all stopped. The sound. The voices. The whole auditorium paused as he waited to hear his sentencing.

No matter what came of it, he had lived his dream: a chance at competing for the title.

Dios. He wanted it now more than ever.

When they announced first place, he didn't react. It was only when Tilda turned to him, eyes wide and shining with tears that it struck him. It was like being electrocuted.

"Alejandro Garcia *y* Mathilda Landrey Garcia!"

He grabbed her then, springing into action. His hands were shaking but he held onto the one woman who hadn't left him, the one woman who had given him the world. His dream.

The audience cheered and the attendants stepped forward. Flowers for Tilda, the plaque for him. Gifts for them both. Everything was in sharp focus: the pictures, colors, people. Suddenly he saw every face, heard every word.

Tears dampened his cheeks. He let them come.

The relief, the joy, trickled out. He could see it in Tilda's eyes, in her smile. This was hers as much as it was his.

They performed on stage as the new world title winners. The performance was transcendental. They moved with a lightness, a joy, a sense of purpose. He truly had everything now: his dreams, his woman, his life back. A second chance. He wasn't going to blow it.

THE PRESS CONFERENCE WAS A FLURRY OF ACTIVITY. A part of him was hyper aware of the camera, the bright lights, the questions; his mind was taking snap shots of everything to sift through later. The other part of him was entrenched in the moment. His head was swimming; he was drunk on the win, and he wanted to ride that sensation until the sun came up.

"Congratulations! How did you feel you performed through the competition?"

"Strong. We've been dancing together, working with ways we can interpret the music, trying to extend ourselves for years now. I think this is proof it's paid off."

"That and he's a slave driver for perfection." Tilda nudged him.

Alé threw his arm around her shoulder, bringing her in. It felt good to laugh. To be free of that pressure.

"It certainly has—but tell us, what were your thoughts on seeing your ex, Camila Morales, here tonight as the guest judge?"

He kept his voice measured, even as his back tensed. "It was a surprise. But Camila is very good at what she does. We wish her the best."

"No hard feelings there? You winning the title when she came in runner up?"

"You'll have to ask Camila that."

"Keeping a tight lip."

"I think tonight is more about our dancing and the future," Tilda added. "It's something we hoped for, but you never really expect to win. Not with all the other amazing dancers out tonight."

"Well said. And what are the plans after tonight?"

"Take a week off! Back to Melbourne where we have our studio and back on the dance floor!" Alé grinned. "This is our life. Teaching, possibly touring. What we really want to do is show others the layers of this dance. Whether you're a beginner, wanting to perfect your *adornos*, or even a couple wanting to compete, we aim to guide others and show them the heart of tango."

"And hopefully have them fall in love with it like we did."

"We can't wait to see it. And you both back in Buenos Aires again. Congratulations!"

"Thank you! You can't keep us away…especially not with these gorgeous shoes!" Tilda flicked out one foot encased in a pair of bold red *Commes*.

Alé smiled, remembering her reaction to receiving her first pair. It felt like another lifetime ago. Now she had a whole cupboard full. After tonight's win, she'd have a ton more.

Once the interviews were over, and with a promise to see their friends, George and Betty, at the hotel later, Alé turned to Tilda.

"I'm so proud of you." She kissed him lightly on the lips.

"Likewise. My Tilda. A *Mundial de Tango* Champ."

She laughed, joy ringing out loud and clear.

"I want to take you home. Celebrate the win. But first, champagne. I'll meet you in the dressing room?"

"I won't argue with that."

ALÉ CLENCHED THE BOTTLE IN HIS HAND. THE WEIGHT of it kept him grounded, even though the space around him tilted. He was about to storm into the room when Tilda turned.

He stepped out of her line of sight, watching through the open wedge of the door. In the mirrored reflection his past and future collided. He wanted to step between them, to protect her, but if history taught him anything, his woman didn't need it.

Tilda paused, then turned slowly. "You've got some nerve showing up here."

She was greeted with a cat-like shrug, sly and slow. "That's no way to speak to the guest judge, is it?"

"Please don't tell me you're trying to convince me you're responsible for our win."

Camila studied her nails. "I have a lot of power in this place."

"That's what you think. Others would call it a dangerous delusion."

The sneer flashed fast, then disappeared.

"Listen, *mija*, every time you look back on this day, you'll think of me. I *am* responsible for that win. And I'll always be a part of his success. You think you amateurs would have placed without me?"

Tilda's laughter was incredulous. "Get a grip, Camila.

You're so full of yourself. We won this without the delusional behaviour of a tango has-been. Why did you bother coming here? To be a third wheel in our success? That's sad, even for you."

"My, my, the little kitten has claws."

Tilda stalked over.

Alé's hand hovered at the door handle. He didn't think she would strike out, but he couldn't be sure about Camila. The woman was unstable, coming here after all these years.

"Let's set the record straight, shall we? You're a guest judge. A bullshit title they give to wannabe, D-list dancers who need to jump from one reality dance show to the next, trying to make ends meet. You have no clout here except what lies you tell yourself in your head.

"The judges, the *real* judges, made the decision. And guess what? We won the title. So you can go around telling yourself you had some kind of clout, but we know the truth.

"You're desperate and a narcissist and one day all those wiles you use to get ahead won't work anymore, Camila. So let me give you a piece of advice my *husband* gave you years ago. Leave. Don't ever come near us again. You're not welcome. What's more…" Tilda leaned in close, whispered. "Whatever games you're playing, won't work. Alé and I are solid."

Alé shoved open the door and had the satisfaction of watching Camila jump.

"You heard my wife. Leave."

She turned, smile faltering for a split second. "I came to congratulate the happy couple." She shrugged, seemingly nonchalant, but the gesture came off sulky.

"Like hell you were. Get out before I call security."

"She was just leaving."

Alé searched Tilda's sweet face, but all he saw was determination.

"Weren't you?"

Before Camila had a chance to spread her poison, Tilda ushered her out, locking the door for good measure.

Alé hugged her. To give comfort or receive it, he wasn't so sure.

"You okay?"

"I'm more than okay. The nerve of that woman…though I guess I shouldn't be surprised. Alé, tonight isn't about the past. It isn't about Camila or the accident or even what it all means. Tonight is about us, what we've achieved. We did it. World champs. And it's because of you: the man who never gave up. On me. On our love. So, tonight is for celebrating. Let's just enjoy the now. We have forever to decide what happens next."

"You know that I ask myself, what did I do to deserve this woman?"

"Oh, I dunno. But I do know what you can do to show me your appreciation."

The pressure on Alé's chest had dissipated. He couldn't seem to stop smiling. "I think I can handle that, Mrs. Garcia."

"Handle away."

"But first, a toast. To us."

"One world champ to another."

He opened the bottle, pouring them each a glass before taking a sip of his champagne. Then with a flick of his wrist, Alé tipped the contents of his glass over her chest.

The squeal of protest cut through any remaining tension.

"Alé!"

"Sorry."

"Like hell you are, you rat." She laughed then gasped when

he bent his head to suck the drops off her collarbone, her breast. "Alejandro Garcia. If I didn't know any better, I'd say this was planned."

"Mmm. I don't know what you're talking about. But I do know that this dress is soaking wet."

He swept his tongue up her neck to the underside of her ear. "What say we get you out of it?"

Her moan of approval was all the answer he needed.

Peeling off her dress, he uncovered her flushed skin. He let the material gather at her waist, walking her back to the high bench that ran alongside the mirror.

Unsnapping the press studs between her legs, he drew up the material, exposing the smooth skin beneath.

With her dress half undone, her pussy exposed, he placed her up on the table. Then he feasted.

He licked the circle of her belly button, nipping the smooth, soft skin beneath until he reached her clit. He stopped to breathe her in. She was sweet and ripe, enough to whet his appetite.

The sounds she made, her sighs and groans, guided him. He licked at the sensitive flesh, first long slow strokes, then shorter, circular movements that had her hips launching off the bench. He held her thighs, diving his tongue inside her. Fucking her with his mouth.

She ground against his tongue now, tits bouncing with each undulation.

He was rock hard, but he wanted her to come. To lose control completely. He wanted to taste her when she did.

Tilda's breathing grew shallow. Her moans louder.

It was the sweetest sound in the world. To give her this. To please her.

"Oh…Alé! I'm going to…"

He kept the pace, sensing her release. And then it happened. She jerked her hips, and grabbed his hair, before coming. He increased the pressure, feeding off her moans until he felt her shatter again.

With shaking fingers, he opened the zipper of his trousers.

"I want to come on your tits. Will you let me fuck you?"

"Yes, Alé. Fuck me, now."

He kissed her, thrusting, dueling, showing her how he wanted her.

With a groan, he pulled back, dragging her to the edge of the table, pushing her against the smooth, hard surface. Dress gathered at her waist, body and face flushed, he thrust inside.

"Oh!"

This was how he wanted her. Loved to see her. Spread before him. Tousled and aroused. And his. To take. To fuck. To please.

"You like this?"

He rocked back and forth, the rhythmic pace setting his teeth on edge. Her moans made him harder than ever.

"Yes…"

"In Spanish."

"*Si*, Alé. *Cógeme más fuerte.*"

"*Dios.*"

His body took over. He pounded into her wet pussy. He loved hearing the sound.

"*Si. Fuerte.*"

"*Fuerte*? Like this?"

"Oh…I—"

The look on her face, the way her body responded to him, broke him, and any restraint he had left.

He fucked her now, chasing his pleasure. He watched her tits bounce, felt her hot and wet around him. He was buried so deep inside her, he could feel her tight and slick. He was getting drenched and knew she was close.

"Let go, Mathilda. I want you to drench my cock."

And seconds later, she was shuddering. The warmth on his cock as she squirted, drove him fucking wild. He kept the pressure, with hard, quick thrusts, as she screamed his name. She had lost complete control, succumbing to her orgasm.

And in doing so, called to his own.

"Come for me, Alé." Tilda's voice coaxed him, urged him to let go.

Alé pumped, blind to all else. He was sweaty, his heart thumping, his muscles tight. The sound of her pussy, slippery and wet, as he thrust into her was enough to make him lose control. And when the familiar rushing release powered through him, he pulled out. Shouting her name, he came, hard, on her tits.

His orgasm was powerful. All encompassing. It was always that way whenever she squirted. It turned him on. Drove him a little crazy. As it was new to both of them, he was still thrilled by it.

He couldn't do anything but slump against her now, crushing her against the table. After a few minutes, he slowly inched back up, taking her with him. He placed a kiss on her nose.

"We need to start having more horizontal sex." Tilda pushed aside a loose strand of hair. Her cheeks were flushed, her eyes heavy and satisfied. He never got tired of seeing her like this.

"Maybe we just have really hot vertical sex? I remember a

certain bookshelf that was christened a few years ago now, *wife*."

"Well, *husband*," she murmured, "one day you're going to get caught with your pants down."

"Something tells me I don't think you would mind if I did."

CHAPTER FOUR

HE WAS A KING RETURNING TO HIS CASTLE. IN SOME ways, the dance floor always would be his home. They'd be on a plane again all too soon, touring and teaching internationally, but for now, he would enjoy being home with his friends and tango family. He had said goodbye to his mother and sister back in Buenos Aires, certain they would see him again soon enough.

The reception they received at Gus' celebration *milonga* a week later was something else. Streams of dancers offered their congratulations, many having watched their performance through a live stream.

The satisfaction, the unbelievable high since coming back to Australia, hadn't faded. It seemed like they were in a neverending party, with dance schools already contacting him across the states and territories, not to mention the international buzz.

Finally, it was happening. The career he wanted made real because of one woman.

Taking Tilda's hand, he planted a kiss on the small palm.

He owed her his life. He had the satisfaction of seeing her face light up, before they were distracted by another couple with well wishes.

They mingled with friends and students, making their way through the crowded *milonga*.

"There's our favorite designer!" Alé kissed Amira on both cheeks.

"Congratulations! Again! You must be so thrilled."

"I think we won on the dress alone. I wasn't the only man who was turned on by it."

"Ew. That's kind of gross."

Tilda nudged him in the ribs, laughing. "Ignore him. Though I have to say, the dress did get a ton of compliments. I gave people your business card."

Amira frowned. "But I don't have a business card."

"Tilda wrote your details on the back of ours. I hope you have a good physiotherapist on call for all the sewing you'll be doing. You'll be needing an assistant by the end of the month."

Amira's mouth opened. "What?"

Tilda squeezed her arm. "I told you I'm not the only one who loves your designs. We've a dozen *tangueras* wanting you to design for them too, and as we'll be touring again, I'll need just as many dresses for our shows."

The smile on Amira's face was like a beacon.

Alé was struck. "Did you cut your hair?"

She raised her eyebrows, running her hands through the shoulder-length waves. "Err…no. Does it look like it?"

Alé glanced at Tilda. "There's something different about her, *no*?" He caught his wife's 'don't pry' stare but pressed on. "I'm serious. There is something about you tonight. Something has changed since we last saw you."

Amira opened her mouth then shrugged. "Can't think of anything." She glanced over his shoulder.

"Waiting for someone?"

"Sorry, I'm being rude. I was just…no, I'm not."

But her eyes flicked to the right, then the left. Definitely looking for someone.

"Actually, Alé, I think you might be right. There is something different about you, Amira. You're…glowing. If I didn't know any better, I'd say you met someone."

"Eh? That fast? We go to Buenos Aires and Amira finds herself a *tanguero*? Who is the lucky guy?"

"Who's who?" A sultry voice drifted from behind them.

Tilda squealed, turning to throw herself into Isabella's arms.

"Izzy! I'm so happy you came!"

"And miss the fancy party in your honour? Uh, no." She kissed Tilda before turning to Alé. "You bloody *culo*, not ringing me to tell me immediately! I had to watch replays along with all the other shleps."

"It's not his fault, Izzy, we had a spot of…interference."

Brown eyes rounded in surprise. "Ooh goss! Do share. Hello, Amira, *chicka*! Your dress has been getting rave reviews."

"So I've been told."

"And I'm still keen on those practice pants I spoke to you about. These legs were made for show."

Alé and Tilda answered. "We know."

Isabella swatted him. "Don't be rude. I'm going to Buenos Aires in a few months, so I want to look my best. God knows I need a bloody break what with choreographing the *Mundial* and work, I won't have any energy left to actually enjoy the tango."

"The *milongas* there are drawing some great dancers. You won't come back, Isabella."

"Alé, if I could quit my job…actually." Isabella shook her head, curls bouncing. "No I wouldn't. I love interior design too much, but I am looking forward to a break." She waved a hand between them. "Enough about me. *So.*" She turned to Amira. "Who is the lucky man you speak of?"

"We've been grilling our dear Amira about her love life. Alé and I have a suspicion she's fallen head over heels for a *tanguero.*"

Isabella cut a disinterested glance around the room. "These lot? Hardly. Not worth the time."

"For you, Isabella. But our Amira is not old and cynical."

"Speak for yourself, Alé. And I'm not cynical. Just realistic. Unless there's someone new on the scene. Or an international dancer."

"What about Keith? Has he stolen your heart, dear Amira?" Alé teased, nudging her.

"Oooh no, it has to be Gus!" Tilda giggled.

"Pay no attention to these idiots." Isabella flicked back her hair. "It's slim pickings here. She could do better than this lot."

"What about Sebastian?"

"Sebastian Galvett?" Isabella rolled her eyes so hard, he was afraid they'd pop out of her skull. "Sebastian wouldn't bother. No offense, Amira, but that man is so full of himself he'd just as soon walk by you as ask you to dance."

Alé winked at Tilda. He loved nothing more than teasing Isabella. And Sebastian was her kryptonite.

"Don't be too hard on the guy. He's had it rough, since his sister's death."

"That's a long time for him to be an asshole."

Tilda shook her head. "All those rumors about him being responsible has got to wear thin by now. To carry that blame around for her death is just awful. Gus said he hasn't been the same since. And he knew them both."

"That doesn't improve my opinion of him. And it doesn't excuse him being a dick. I wouldn't be offended if he doesn't ask you to dance, Amira, darling."

"I don't really know Sebastian," she proffered.

"That is a problem I can fix." Alé raised his hand. Through the crowd, the man in question nodded back. Eventually, Sebastian placed his drink down and wandered over.

The sound of disgust in the back of Isabella's throat was satisfying. It was like grilling his baby sister.

"Congratulations, Alejandro. Mathilda."

"Thanks. Hey, have you've met Amira? She's the talented dressmaker who designed our winning outfits."

Sebastian nodded to her, then barely glanced at Isabella. Interesting.

"*Qué pasa?*"

They spoke for a few minutes about the win, dancing in Buenos Aires, life in general.

When a man came to ask Tilda to dance, Alé turned to Amira. "Care to tango?"

She nodded, distracted.

"Maybe you two might want to dance too?" Alé grinned, looking from Sebastian back to Isabella.

"Thank you, no. I'm not dancing."

"You come to a *milonga* and not dance, Seb?"

"It's just as legitimate as coming to one and gossiping."

Alé stepped to the side, motioning for Sebastian to join him. "Buddy, Isabella is an amazing dancer."

"I have no desire to dance with the village bicycle, Alejandro. Leave it alone."

Alé's back stiffened. "Watch your mouth. Isabella is a very good friend."

Sebastian ran a hand over his face. "Sorry, that was rude."

"But not unexpected." Isabella shoved between them. "Or unheard. Take your cat's ass attitude and piss off, Sebastian. No one wants your shit opinion here."

Isabella stormed off.

Alé studied the pained expression on Sebastian's usually stoic face.

"Too far, buddy."

"I know it. I'm sorry for it."

"Useless apologizing to me, it's Isabella who needs to hear it. And there'll be groveling involved if you want it accepted. What's going on? Is it about—

"Leave it, Alejandro. Not tonight. Please, not tonight."

And then it dawned on him. Sebastian's haggard appearance: the dark stubble, haunted eyes, it was like looking back at an old photo of himself. Of a time when the ghosts shadowed his every move. A time before Tilda.

The anniversary. *Her* anniversary.

He placed a hand on his arm even as Sebastion flinched. "*Madre de Dios*. Sebastian, go home, get away from all this. It's not good to be reminded."

"It's my penance. It's exactly where I need to be."

"Not here. Trust me when I say you're no good to anyone like this. I've been there. Go home."

Sebastian rubbed at the scruff on his cheek. Eventually, he nodded.

Alé watched him walk slowly through the crowd. He

would pay him a visit in the morning, with some food and aspirin. Experience told him the man would need it.

"WHAT ARE WE DOING HERE, ALÉ?"

It was late, well past midnight, but he knew he didn't want to go home just yet.

"I was feeling nostalgic."

Tilda frowned. "So you brought us back to the studio?"

"*Sí*. I wanted to return to where it all began."

They climbed the stairs of the dance studio they owned, the place where they met, argued, fell in love. The light of the moon guided them as they crossed the rectangular space. Taking their time, they climbed the second set of stairs that led to their private room.

Tilda reached for the switch, but Alé covered her hand with his own.

"Tonight is for moonlight. For candlelight. For romance."

Taking his time, eyes adjusting to darkness, Alé found the candles, lighting them carefully. The upstairs area was once sparse, with the bare minimum of furnishings. It now held small details: the vase of geraniums on the low table, a throw placed on a new love seat. Evidence that his life had changed, elements of the woman who changed it.

Cupping her face, he swallowed his emotions. "I want to paint you."

Tilda's laugh was filled with embarrassment. "But you've already painted me. In fact, you have *dozens* of paintings. A ton of sketches."

"No." He kissed her face, the tip of her nose, the corner of her lips. "I want to paint you naked. In the moonlight."

A faint blush spread across her skin. He loved that she still reacted to him this way. It filled him with an overwhelming urge to hold her. Protect her.

"Alé."

"Will you let me?"

"You know I can never refuse. Not when you look at me like that."

He sensed her arousal. It was a whisper, a tantalizing call, but he let it hang in the air. Close and heady, to take when he was ready.

He guided her to the love seat and took a moment to stroke, tease, give her pleasure.

Alé brushed his lips along the delicate line of her collarbone, teasing the thin strap of her gown down, past her hips until it pooled on the floor.

"So beautiful."

Tilda unclipped her hair, brushing it back. It was long now, fanning out past her breasts, down her waist. Before she could fidget, he took her hands, placing kisses in each palm. He stroked her hips, then removed her bra.

Unable to stop himself, he cupped one breast, pinching the nipple before replacing his hand with his mouth. When he heard her breathing quicken, he drew back, afraid he was going to lose control. He was bound to her, caught up in every flicker of emotion. He wanted to give her everything, the moon in the sky if he could.

Slipping off her panties, he let them pool at her feet before guiding her to the love seat.

"How am I meant to sit? It feels awkward lounging naked and well…"

"You're perfect. Just relax. Watch me, talk to me about how Dex is managing the new release at the store."

She rolled her eyes, violet now and shimmering. "I know what you're trying to do."

"Then humour me, *mi corazón*."

He swung her legs across the side of the chair. When she crossed them over, he nodded in approval. He placed one arm casually across her belly.

"Only because you look so pretty."

"*Gracias*, wife."

"*De nada*, husband."

He groaned. "I love when you talk Spanish."

"I know." She sent him a sly wink, tracing her lips with her tongue.

"I also know what you're trying to do here, and it's not going to distract me."

"It was worth a try."

Her laughter crossed the space between them, and his heart soared. He never tired of listening to it.

Gradually, he noted the shift in her shoulders, the way her body sank into the seat, and he knew he had found that moment.

He set up quickly, wanting to capture her beauty, her serenity. Her skin in the moonlight was exactly the image he had wanted to paint, smooth as porcelain, soft as silk. And those eyes, ones that looked back at him now, were filled with trust.

Her face grew animated, deep in her discussion of the books on order.

She was his light. He needed nothing else in the world except his woman, preferably naked, with the soft candlelight cupping her body, the moonlight dancing over all that pale skin.

His heart caught, trembled. He fell in love with her over and over again.

Alé still couldn't believe his luck. The woman he almost lost was now his wife.

He found another shade he needed, dipping his brush. Quick fevered strokes covered the blank page. There was an urgency now, to have her, to take all that emotion that swirled inside him, to show her what she meant to him.

He painted like a man possessed. The curves, the angles of her body, all stoked the fire inside him.

He found the light, gave into the moment until the shapes began to resemble a face, a limb, his lover.

"Alé? Can I see?"

He stood back, shook out the cramp in his hand.

"It's not ever going to do you justice. But it is in your likeness."

Tilda stood, crossing to him. The short intake of breath was all the confirmation he needed. She turned then, a look of surprise on her face.

"Alé." She swallowed.

"Don't." He took her in his arms. "No tears. My heart, it can't take it."

"Happy tears. You've painted me generously."

"Truthfully. It's how I see you."

"Glowing?" She raised an eyebrow and God help him, he found it sexy as hell.

"It's inside you. This…what's the word…aura. It's how you are. How I see you. But tell me, are you happy?"

She cupped his face. "Where is this coming from?"

"I need to know. These past few months have been a blur, and now we've won the world title, things will change. I want to be sure you want this life. That you're happy with me."

"More than happy. Nothing is meant to stay the same forever."

"Things will get busier…"

"I don't mind busy. Alé, I've been wanting this life. The bookstore, tango, now this title, I've wanted this all with you."

"*Bueno*. I wanted to be sure. To check in."

"Consider me checked."

When goosebumps raced along her chest, he drew her closer.

"I think it's time you let me show you how much I appreciate you."

Her laughter, soft, welcoming, floated between them.

"I won't complain."

He drew her to the bed, spreading the soft silk throw across the covers, laying her down gently. Tonight was for stoking the flames, for sweet and slow. His heart thudded. Her hands, small and skilled, drew his clothes off, stroking, sweeping over him.

He brushed his thumb over her bottom lip, red and swollen from his kisses. When she drew the tip in her mouth and sucked, his body burned.

Tilda pushed him back on the bed, straddling him. Her mouth explored his, then inched lower, until it found him hard and straining.

The soft sensation of her mouth on his cock, the heat and

suction, was pure bliss. No matter how many times they made love, fucked, had sex, she never failed at driving him insane. Like every time was the first.

He groaned when one breast brushed against his leg. Looking down, he watched as she sucked him, the steady rhythm more potent than any *tanda*, more arresting than any song.

The combination of her soft body against his, and the pressure building in his balls, nearly broke his control. Drawing her up, he brushed back her hair.

"Not like that."

Positioning herself over him, she lowered herself down, a delicious homecoming.

Tilda began slowly, drawing out his arousal, playing with herself until her movements quickened, the pace increasing.

Seeing her pleasure, hearing her moans, only spurred him on further—he needed to come but wanted to linger, to draw it out. Focusing on the candlelight, he steadied his breathing then looked back at the woman above him.

She was a temptress. A lover. A friend. And the one person in the whole world who could see beneath the surface. The one woman who knew him. Accepted him completely.

He watched her now, entranced. Breasts bouncing, body undulating, the look on her face was one he never tired of. He gave that to her. And in giving her pleasure, sought so much of his own.

"You have to stop or I'll come. Tilda..."

He held her hips.

"Do it, Alé."

He searched her blue eyes for clarity. To make sure he understood her correctly.

"But I don't have any—"

"I know. There's nothing between us now. I want this. Come, Alé. Come inside me."

The words, the meaning behind them, filled him. The adrenaline, the power that coursed throughout his body, was unlike anything he had experienced before. His arousal was burning hot. For her. For their future. He could never deny her requests. He could never deny her anything.

With slow thrusts, he watched her. "Ladies first."

When her breathing shattered, shallow gasps marking her orgasm, Alé let go. Groaning, he pumped into her. He clenched her hips now, fingers digging in as he filled her. There was nothing between them. No barrier. No restraint. It was the greatest turn on.

He was whole, sated, complete.

When he saw the slow, satisfied curve of her mouth, he sighed. Relieved. "Happy?"

"Very."

Alé drew her to him. With the moonlight shining through the windows and the woman he loved in his arms, he felt like the luckiest bastard in the world.

He stroked her back, hugging her close, happier than he thought possible. He could see their future, where it would lead. Finally, he was home.

Alé drifted off, body and mind at ease. Heart full.

All he felt was her embrace. All he heard was her voice. All he knew, was Tilda.

SECRETS AND SCANDALS

SWEET, SEXY, SCANDALOUS BOOK 3

A Sweet,
Sexy,
Scandalous
Series

Secrets
and
SCANDALS
~ BOOK THREE ~

IDA BRADY

CHAPTER ONE

Isabella Diaz was restless and aroused, a combination that never failed to put her in a bad mood. It was well past midnight, and the *milonga* was a heavy throb of beautiful people, in beautiful clothes, dancing beautifully. She may as well be watching paint dry.

Instead of cutting her losses and heading back to her apartment, she waited. She was in the mood for something different; what that was, she wasn't certain. But she figured that the 2:00AM crowd, the *milongueros* who lived and breathed the type of tango danced in the middle of the night with strangers, would be the distraction she had been craving of late. Even if her gut was telling her otherwise.

Her gut could go straight to hell for all she cared.

Buenos Aires was renowned for its all-night dance halls, promiscuous men, and little *media lunas* served at dawn, to wash away the acrid taste of loneliness that coaxed many out to the *milongas* in the dead of night.

Normally, dancing was a way to burn through all her

energy, except tonight she was dissatisfied with everyone around her.

She had been looking forward to this holiday, to taking a break from the clients, the choreography, the million and one other hats she wore back home. But now she was here, she felt lost. After the first week, she blamed it on the jet lag, her fatigue. After the second, it was the late nights, living like a vampire only to emerge for the odd brunch with friends. But by the third week, when the tears had come, sudden and strong, waking her in the middle of the morning, she accepted the problem. It was her.

Not caring one bit for the sudden melancholy, Isabella threw herself into her holiday, dancing, drinking, and a few times hooking up with a woman or two at the queer tango clubs. Anything to stop the echo reverberating through her soul. It had been building, for most of her life she had been avoiding it, covering up that loss, desperate to consume anything that made her feel alive. But it followed her around in some form ever since she was little, ever since she could understand what had happened. She dared not give into the gaping chasm.

The restlessness, the sense that something wasn't right in her life, appeared whenever she had the chance to sit still, so she became a blur of activity. Even though she was only in Argentina for a relatively short trip, she had already moved the furniture, bought a few plants and throws and made the space in the rental apartment her own. The curse of being an interior designer.

Isabella had been searching for something more, ever since she arrived in Buenos Aires. Like many of the other lost souls that fell in love with tango, she was yearning for the ultimate. The pinnacle. A connection. *Un abrazo*.

She had danced with many men and women. She had led, followed, and choreographed her way through tango, always eager for a new experience. Even though it had been exhilarating at times, she knew, deep down to her three-inch, blood red *Commes*, that something big was waiting for her. She had yet to experience the drugging pull that only dancing with a truly magnetic leader could offer.

She wanted it. Craved it. Dreamed about it more than she cared to admit.

Whilst she could break down the steps of the tango, *milonga*, and *vals* to the bare mechanics, no amount of choreography could replace the sublime sensation of being consumed by the dance. By the lead. Because even though she enjoyed leading, tonight she wanted to be led. To close her eyes and allow a man—tonight was for dancing with men—to give her pleasure.

Despite her bad mood, Isabella was caught by the cat-like grace of a particular couple, their movements slow but sensual, drawing out every beat until it looked like the music was written solely for them. As they made another revolution around the floor, she stiffened. Isabella's sound of distress was a mix between a groan and a squeak.

The quick lick of panic whipped her heart rate up as if she had just danced a frenetic *milonga*. Instead, she sat at the edge of the dance floor, the dark shadows shrouding her but revealing *him*, the man she loathed, in a halo of light.

What the bloody bitching hell was Sebastian Galvett doing in Buenos Aires? Looking like a million dollars in that tailored suit, no less. Open neck collar. Clean shaven jaw. And an utter bastard.

More importantly, why in God's good name was he walking over?

SEBASTIAN WAS BORED AS FUCK. HE HAD BEEN LIBERATED enough to allow his friend to bring him to *Tanda Finale* for another late-night dance in the city that never slept. New York had nothing on the die-hard *tangueros* of Buenos Aires: the 2:00AM boys out for a *tanda*, and the lecherous ones for a bit of T&A. Not that he could blame them. Tango women—especially tourists—were often lulled by the Argentine men. A few whispered words, a couple of spins around the floor, and the women were inevitably putty in their hands. Something for them to run back home and tell their girlfriends all about.

Sebastian fought against the bitter memories that threatened to snarl and snap like some rabid animal. Some people never had that luxury of returning home. Clamping down on the intrusive thoughts, and the helplessness that followed, Sebastian walked further through the *milonga*. He couldn't think about her now.

He assessed the room, analyzing the women dancing, their technique and response to the music. He didn't want to suffer through another mediocre *tanda* with some tourist who looked a million bucks but couldn't move. He had made that mistake all those years ago, when he was just learning how to dance.

So much of tango was steeped in pain. It was pleasurable and heartbreaking to continue to come to *milongas*, to dance socially and find that he loved and hated being on the floor in equal measure. Didn't the Germans have a word for that? Or maybe it was the Japanese…The only word he could think of in English was fucked.

That's what he was, what he had been for the past six years. Not in a getting jiggy-with-it way, either. Though, he'd had his fair share of one-nighters, two-nighters, hell, even week-long sex benders during that time. None of it took away the heavy, oppressive weight that stalked him once it was over. No matter what he did, he couldn't escape it.

But he had made a promise a lifetime ago. One which he intended to keep. His pain was a penance of sorts. One he would bear for the rest of his life.

Sebastian threaded through the heaving crowds of people, some milling along the wall in discussion, others seated at the circular tables. When he had given up on finding someone to dance with, he headed towards the bar. That's when he spotted her.

A woman who infuriated him with just a glance. A woman whom he swore he wouldn't touch, but one who compelled him to all the same. He didn't believe it was Fate that they were both in this foreign country at the same time. He didn't believe Fate was real.

But even though his mind warned him to stay put and back the fuck away, his feet carried him across the floor and up to the table where she sat, regal as a queen. Distant as the sea.

"Isabella."

She spared him a flicker beneath her long dark lashes. He ignored the arrow in his gut. His interest in her only annoyed him further.

"Stalking me, Sebastian?"

"I flew thousands of miles across the world just to hover over you at a mediocre *milonga* in Buenos Aires. I can't seem to keep away."

A sneer snuck up her face. If anything, it made her even more compelling. The arrow speared deeper; his interest was very fast turning into desire. He had no time for it.

"Only *you* would think this *milonga* is mediocre, Sebastian." She pushed back a dark curl that had escaped the knot at the base of her neck. "Does nothing ever please you? Or are you always dissatisfied with the world and everyone in it?"

"Not everyone."

She seemed suddenly wary: eyes narrowed, shoulders stiff.

He couldn't understand why he needed to keep his guard up around her. But in the few exchanges they had managed over the years, he always found himself on the cusp of saying or doing something he knew he would regret. Acknowledging that, knowing that she had some bizarre power over him, Sebastian steered well clear.

One tanned, toned shoulder shrugged in derision. She ignored his remark, and the tight ball in his gut seemed to loosen. All the more reason to be wary.

"So what brings you here then, Sebastian?"

"A friend insisted I come and enjoy the spoils of Buenos Aires."

"I didn't know robots could feel."

It wasn't as if the insult was something new. He had heard it before from other women, from some of his male friends too. Yet somehow this woman could say the same thing and it was akin to being stabbed in the back by a thousand sharp knives. Why did he care what she thought of him? Dangerous ground. He was on it, and it was fast turning into quicksand.

Because of it, Sebastian sat beside her, needing to do something, anything, rather than hover. Orange blossom and jasmine surrounded him. He leaned closer, breathing in her scent; it was yet another sort of penance.

He had the distinct pleasure of seeing her shift back in her chair. Good.

"What do you have against me, Isabella?"

"Other than your arrogance and complete and utter disdain for a majority of dancers on the scene...oh I don't know, your sunny personality?"

"I don't dislike new dancers."

"Oh please, you're such a dance snob. You never give anyone new on the scene a look in, preferring to dance with your own little elite crew. And God forbid should someone try something new..." Her dark eyes flashed in derision.

"I don't see a problem preferring traditional tango to *nuevo*." He had made a point of not hiding his opinions either.

"Just because I like vanilla ice cream doesn't mean I won't like choc chip. You won't know unless you try it. And *nuevo* dancers aren't all sloppy as many traditionalists would believe. So they play with the mechanics of the dance? So what if they break with the A-frame and use spins and twirls? They're still dancing the basics of tango."

"How do you know I haven't tried it and hate it?"

"Just a hunch." That feline mouth of hers kicked up in the corners. Her lips were painted a rich, vibrant fire-engine red; he couldn't seem to look away.

"I distinctly remember going to *milongas* when I came on the scene and saw you standing not two feet away from me and not even bothering to ask to dance."

"That was a long time ago. I make an effort to—" His

mouth clamped shut. "I shouldn't have to justify myself to you." He justified himself to nobody.

"Too beneath you, eh?"

"I don't see why I have to make excuses for my preferences. I don't grill you on the types of men you dance with, or the style which you take, do I?" The muscle on his cheek began to twitch. He was allowing her to get to him. *Back the fuck off, Seb.*

"I'm surprised you even notice me or any of the other plebs on the scene. After the way you spoke to me a few months ago, you're lucky I'm even looking at you."

Sebastian ground his teeth together, breathing in very carefully. She poked and prodded at his temper like a wasp, provoking a reaction. If he wasn't careful, he would lose his cool. Life had taught him to keep a clear head, to not give in to his emotions.

Guilt stabbed at his anger, dulling it. "Fair call." He had a brief moment of satisfaction as her head whipped around to face him fully. While her side profile was arresting, she was breathtaking up close. Sebastian lifted his hands in surrender. "I admit, I shouldn't have said it."

"And I quote, 'I have no desire to dance with the village bicycle.' Did I get that right?"

"Isabella—"

"What? You're going to backtrack now?"

"No, I regret what I said. But in fairness, it wasn't meant for your ears."

"So that makes it better?"

Was that sweat? He rolled his shoulders but didn't back away. Was he actually sweating? Alejandro warned him he would have to grovel. His friend wasn't wrong.

"No. It doesn't." He spoke carefully, uncertain of her response. Not that it mattered. He was letting her get under his skin which was never a good sign. "I'm not trying to justify it. I'm saying I shouldn't have said it. I don't think you're the village bike."

"So what if I am? So what if I *have* been around, spreading my legs for every man and woman on the scene? It's none of your business, right?"

Jesus. Images. Sinful images of those long shapely legs spread eagled, wearing nothing but her red heels, hit him with a little too much force.

Sebastian waited a beat before answering. "Look, I said I was sorry. I was in a foul mood and lashed out. Even if you do go around screwing all the men in Buenos Aires, it wouldn't be my business."

"Damn right it isn't…"

"You accept my apology then?"

She shrugged. "We'll see. So why are you here if you refuse to dance with anyone?"

"I never said that. Look, I've danced with plenty of beginners over the years—women and men. But these days I like to dance with the best."

"You've never danced with me, sunshine."

"I don't need to."

"Afraid?" She raised one dark eyebrow. It was sexy as fuck.

Sebastian shook his head even as the words stuck in his throat. "I know we wouldn't get along."

"If your dancing is anything like your personality, I think you might be right." Isabella looked up at the roof of the *milonga*.

"What the hell are you doing?"

"Making sure the Gods don't strike me down. I just agreed with Sebastian Galvett."

"More like Satan."

"I don't believe in the devil."

Sebastian shivered. "You should. Especially in this town. Especially the way you look."

Isabella's face grew serious. He overstepped the mark but couldn't help himself. Not after what happened.

"I can take care of myself."

"That's what a lot of people think. That doesn't mean you shouldn't be careful."

If he could stop it, if he could prevent another woman ending up like Zoey, then he would consider it a win. In a fucked-up kind of way.

Isabella leaned closer and he was immediately drawn to those lips: soft, inviting, and tempting as sin. Whatever fragrance she wore infiltrated through his defenses. There was a reason he maintained his distance; it was better for everyone in the long haul. She was an indulgence he refused to consume.

"What happened to her, Seb?"

"That's none of your—"

"Humor me."

"Why?"

"Because I'm a woman, because I'm staying alone in an apartment. Because I asked."

"Ask me another night and I might tell you."

Sebastian knew he was making a mistake. The tell-tale churning in his gut climbed up his chest and along his temples, turning his body to lava. The woman was fucking infuriating.

"Dance with me."

"Uh-huh."

Sebastian stood, hand outstretched. "Or are you the one afraid now, Ms. Diaz? I'm obligated to dance to this song. It's a promise I made many years ago."

The opening notes of Carlos Di Sarli's *Milonguero Viejo* filtered through the crowd. It found him open, vulnerable, and oddly enough yearning for something he hadn't had in a long while. A sliver of light speared through his cloudy, gray memories.

"If you won't, then I'll find someone who will. But I would never have taken Isabella Diaz for a coward."

He observed the match as it struck, the way her eyes grew round then narrowed as she absorbed the burn.

"I know the game you're playing, Sebastian."

"Do you accept the rules?"

"I haven't decided just yet. But I'm in the mood for something different tonight."

"And I'm it?"

"We'll just have to wait and see. And just for the record, I'm no coward."

"Prove me wrong then. Dance with me."

Her mouth opened. Those soft, stained lips pouted. She struggled to get the words out, and Sebastian was petty enough to take pleasure in the soft flush that spread across her cheeks.

The moment she placed her slender hand in his, he knew he had made the worst mistake of his life. At least, the second worst. The first one proved too harrowing to even recall.

Isabella Diaz may have been his kryptonite, but he would never be her hero.

SHE WAS A FORMIDABLE DANCER, NOT LIGHT AND EASY TO move, nor was she a lead weight. She connected in a way that forced him to rise-up, maintain his axis—to keep them as one. She was exuberant, yet graceful. Precise in her footwork and utterly mesmerizing.

With the lights low and the dance floor crowded, the mood surrounding them was deceptive in its intimacy. And yet the connection between them was unbelievable. He knew she registered it too. Those wide brown eyes were wary. Her expression, always open and direct, was as murky as day-old *mate* tea.

But the way she fit against his body, the contrast between soft, heavy breasts and the hard curve of her waist, had him burning in anticipation.

The moment he held her in his arms, he knew he would wind up fucking her. Images of her riding him until he couldn't think anymore appealed on every level.

But like the music, she was striking, tantalizing. Even her smell, the blossom that came from her bundled-up curls intrigued him.

"I bet you didn't expect this?" He couldn't help but tease her. A small, mean part of him wanted to know she was just as rattled by the connection.

"I—You're a real bastard, aren't you, Sebastian?"

He led her around his body in a *giro*, watching the way her mouth twisted in resignation. "That's all the answer I needed."

When a fast *milonga* began, and her breathing turned shallow, he wanted more. To hear her moan, scream, to break through the smug reserve she seemed to hold for him only.

He had watched her dance many times; it was hard to ignore the bright, buoyant way she whirled through the *milonga*. But when it came to him, she was all ice. Derision. What would it be like to pump into her, injecting life and warmth, until she softened to him? Yielded to him.

He set the pace, one that matched the frenetic layers of the music: piano, violin, *bandoneon*, each with their own part to play. A threesome. And he held her, shared one axis, as their feet moved in time to the rhythm. *Milongas* were a joy to dance to, but with Isabella, it was something else entirely.

He sensed her delight in the way she moved: the playful *adornos*, the seductive trills that fired up every bit of his imagination. It made a man wonder what she would be like in bed.

If he had known dancing with her would be like this, he would never have asked her. How could he go back to what it was before? To dance with anyone else?

Her legs—those never-ending miles of leg—seemed to be at once attached to and free from her body. The way her feet would brush the floor, never breaking form, only for her leg to kick out in playful *boleos* was impressive. Whilst her chest was pressed against his, the *milonga* music meant their waists were twisted in constant motion. She moved as if she were floating across the floor. It was one of the greatest aphrodisiacs he had experienced in a long time.

He wanted more.

When she matched his pace, Sebastian set an even more punishing one. When she matched that, he channeled all his desire into the dance.

For years he had been content, happy enough to function with the bare essentials. Attachment was a dangerous game. Twelve minutes was as long as he would last on the tango floor

—the most amount of time he would spend connecting to another person in public. Unless they were in his bed, then time had no limits. He had no limits, his hunger a constant, unquenchable machine. He wanted, needed more of the flesh. More of the pleasure in his bed, his world. Outside of it, he was stone. Nothing penetrated. Nothing infiltrated.

Except now. Except *her*.

He should walk away. Run. Never to return. Instead, he splayed his hand on the small of her slender back and appreciated the silk material. Like a second skin, it clung to her back, the curve of her bottom. It swayed with her body, teasing all who dared to look. He wanted to rip it from her. To feast.

There was fire and ice in his veins now. It would drive him insane if he tried to quench either thirst. He would have her or go mad with it, but the need would always remain.

"I think we both know where this is heading."

Isabella's look was knowing. There would be no coy responses, no feigned innocence. Like a cool breeze after a heat wave, Sebastian breathed it in. She was refreshing and frustrating. Exactly what he didn't need right now. Still…he wanted her. He'd be damned if he would just let her go without having a taste first.

"Back to your place?" Isabella stayed close to his body even though the music had ended.

"Or yours. I'm an easy man."

"I doubt that very much. But I have plans."

"Change them."

"Why?"

"Because I asked."

As a tango *tanda* began, Isabella lifted her hands, switching positions. He knew what she was asking. Never had he let a woman lead him. He'd tried it many times, mostly with men, but never in public had he ceded control. He looked at her hands: small, manicured, and open, waiting for him to accept.

With a slight nod, Sebastian did.

Her lead was strong, sure. Even though she wore impossibly high heels, she maneuvered them both around the floor with a grace and ease most men couldn't muster. When she displaced his leg, stepping into his thigh, he couldn't decide if he was turned on by her dancing or her body. Both were arousing. Captivating. He wanted to sample more, if only she would agree.

By the end of the *tanda*, he had his answer.

CHAPTER TWO

THEY WALKED BACK TO HER APARTMENT IN RELATIVE silence. Whilst his body was on fire, his mind, that broken, tortured mind of his, was lost in the inky darkness. Every time he walked through the streets of Buenos Aires at night, the memories haunted him: painful images, ones he wanted to shove aside, lurked in every corner. It was not knowing what happened that plagued him. That, and the fact that she may have suffered.

It was a split second, all those years ago. A seemingly innocent decision—one that people make all the time—cost him his world. His peace. He would no longer wake up at ease, happy in the knowledge that his loved ones were alive and well.

Not a day went by that he didn't feel responsible on some level. But that stabbing guilt, whether dulled with whiskey or diluted by a swim in the freezing cold sea, was a disease that he lived with, and with every passing day, it was eroding his spirit.

But that's not what people wanted to hear, especially not

after all these years. They expected him to move on. To have recovered from her disappearance like she was a lost wallet or phone. Six years was long enough to have given up hope. Yet here he was, in the city that robbed him of his best friend, his only sibling. It had been six years of wondering just what happened to his older sister, Zoey. More than long enough for them to have 'buried' her.

The thought of her body rotting away somewhere filled him with impotent rage.

Even though she was gone, he still lived in hope. Every year he returned, demanding the truth, only for the police in this dirty, corrupt city to give him the same bullshit excuses he'd heard before.

In a country plagued by poverty, even their hunger for the American dollar couldn't provide him with an answer; it couldn't conjure flesh from a ghost, which is what his sister was to them: an old ghost, a case file number, a *gringo* who got caught up with the wrong crowd and was murdered. Most likely assaulted. Dumped in some remote part of the country. Or better yet, buried deep in a jungle somewhere.

Orange blossoms and jasmine. The scent circled around him, breaking through the darkness. And just like that, the weight lifted a fraction, chased away by the woman beside him.

"Having second thoughts?" Isabella glanced at him, a genuine expression of concern softening her tone.

"Not a chance."

"You're far away there, Sebastian."

"And now I'm back."

She paused, then placed a hand on his arm, briefly. "If you want to—"

"I don't."

"Okay…it can't be easy to be back."

"It isn't. But you get used to having one foot in the past and one in the present."

"Seems to me you're never fully anywhere. Never wholly in one place."

He was struck by the shrewd comment. By her. "That's right."

"Not an easy feat."

"It's excruciating." It rushed out of his mouth, surprising them both. His immediate instinct was to snatch it back, but Isabella's presence made his confession seem like a natural part of the conversation, not an unwelcome blunder.

"If you're not careful you'll become a ghost to everyone around you. And trust me when I say that's far worse."

"What—"

"I can't even begin to say I understand, I don't. But for what it's worth, I'm sorry you're carrying that shit around."

He let it pass, whatever it was that lurked in the shadows wasn't something she wanted to share. He could understand that all too well.

Sebastian affected shock. "Isabella? Sorry? I think you've been letting the *mate* tea get to your head."

"Consider it my one good deed for the day."

"I'd rather a lot less considering and more doing."

"Perfect. Let's go fuck."

"Now you're talking."

Her laughter chased away the remaining darkness, and for the first time in six years he genuinely smiled. It was an odd sensation, but he found that it was not an unwelcome one.

SHE MUST HAVE LOST HER DAMN MIND TO BRING HIM back to her apartment. Hell, to agree to this at all. She hated him. Loathed him. But heaven help her, she wanted him now more than ever.

Long ago she made it her mission to always get what she wanted. She wouldn't be denied this pleasure. Or him. Even if that meant suffering the consequences the next morning.

"There's champagne and fruit in the fridge so help yourself. I keep this apartment pretty well stocked."

"Nice part of town."

"I don't skimp on life's luxuries. And before you start, I've lived in my fair share of backpacker hostels, and in my line of work, you appreciate a bit of luxury."

"Did I say anything?"

"You didn't need to."

"Sounds like justification to me for all this spending."

Isabella shrugged off her irritation before it took hold. She would not be lectured, by *him* of all people, about frivolities of spending. But she had a wicked tongue, and for the life of her just couldn't keep silent. She whirled around to confront him.

Her eyes narrowed. "You son of a bitch, you're goading me."

His grin said it all. "Guilty."

"Wise guy. I could kick you out for being a dick."

Sebastian hauled her against him. Muscle, and a tell-tale hardening at his crotch cut through her annoyance.

"You won't. Not when it's my dick that you're after."

"You really are a smug bastard, aren't you?"

"Like attracts like, isn't that what they say?"

"So is 'better the devil you know.'"

"But you don't know me. Not yet anyway."

"Maybe not ever."

"Are you backing out of this, Isabella? A retreat?"

She assessed his cool green eyes through her own fiery haze. She wanted to wipe that arrogant smile off his face. To claw and scratch at his superior attitude, just as much as she wanted to fuck him.

But she had caught a glimpse of his vulnerability. It seemed she was stupid enough to let it soften her attitude to him. Big mistake. Shit happens in life to a lot of people. It didn't excuse him from being a dick.

When he grabbed her ass, she couldn't help but gasp. His hands—large and confident—were on her, whetting her appetite. But she wanted more than just a taste. She was ravenous for the whole lot, to feast, like a woman starved until she had her fill.

There'd be no going back, something he knew all too well. Bastard.

She ran her fingers down the hard wall of muscle at his abdomen until she cupped his cock through his trousers. He was hard alright. And just as eager as she. Good.

"Not a chance, Sebastian. I'm promised a night of hedonistic pleasure, and I'm more than willing and ready to be fucked."

"I'll have you begging before the night is over."

"We'll see about that."

"Shut the hell up and—"

"Kiss me."

A devilish grin crossed his handsome face before he devoured her. Dancing with him, finding that connection with the one man she couldn't stand, was thrilling and dangerous. She was not prepared for what sex with Sebastian Galvett would be like.

Electric bolts of energy clashed and wrestled for control. Neither would concede. Like clouds before the storm, heavy, expectant, Isabella absorbed his kiss and returned her own with equal fervor.

It was like being electrocuted. Her nipples were almost painfully in need of attention. He shifted, stroking her pussy through her satin underwear. She was hot and needy and so fucking aroused she thought she'd die on the spot. Isabella trembled instead, her tongue wrestling with his in hot, reckless kisses that reached boiling point. She wrenched backwards, afraid for one wild moment that she would come in his arms.

Sebastian steadied her; those ridiculously skilled hands gripped her waist. His eyes were now a dark mossy green.

"There's something I need to tell you." She tried to steady her breathing.

"It can wait."

The peal of the doorbell broke through the current around them.

"I'm afraid it can't." The doorbell chimed again. "That's her now."

She moved like a cat. Sinuous. Sexy. Confident.

"You never told me you were expecting someone."

"You never asked. You just assumed that I would change my plans to accommodate you." Isabella looked back at him, a slow, satisfied smile on her face, then opened the door.

She greeted a woman with a shock of pink and black hair. Their interaction was steeped in warmth and affection.

"Rilla. *Llegas tarde.*"

Rilla rolled her eyes. "You foreigners forget you're on Argentinian time now. We are *always* late. Was your pussy impatient?" She leaned forward, placing a lingering kiss on Isabella's lips.

"I'm so patient, they're thinking of making me a saint."

"You have to be dead for that, don't you?" Sebastian called out.

"You can stop praying, Sebastian. I won't be dropping dead anytime soon." Isabella closed the door, following Rilla into the room.

"Shame. You'd make a great martyr."

Ignoring him, Isabella ran an arm down her friend's back. "Sebastian, this is Rilla. The woman I had a date with tonight."

"A date?"

"A sex date." Rilla interjected.

"I met her at a tango queer club, and we've been *catching up* recently."

Isabella's friend—lover—moved with a different kind of energy. She shrugged out of her jacket, throwing it on the floor, muscles flaring, tattoos on display. She was intriguing, but not as striking. At least not to him. He would have been more than happy to have Isabella to himself tonight, but…

He was a man after all.

One whose appetite was all but demanding to be sated.

"I hope it's okay that Sebastian joins us." Isabella glanced at Rilla.

She connected them all. But then she was always like that.

Even back home he had noticed the way she infiltrated all the different groups of dancers, talking to a range of people across the tango scene. She practically knew everyone. Once upon a time, he did too.

Rilla shrugged, playing with the tongue ring in her mouth. "Suit yourself. I'm not adverse to a bit of dick, but I'm always happy to offer a fist or two if McBroody here isn't packing."

"And why do you assume I'm not packing?"

"I've met a lot of tourists, a lot of men who talk big, look big, but don't have the goods to back it up."

"I'm sorry to disappoint you then, but I've not had any complaints about my…package."

Sebastian fought not to stare at the shockingly pink, chin-length swing of hair, the soft femme clothes in contrast to the heavy liner around her eyes and tattoos on her arms.

"We'll find out soon enough. I know you both thought it would be vanilla tonight, but I'm in the mood for scissoring *and* cock. Is this going to be a problem?" Isabella turned to him, as if daring him to protest.

"A threesome is every red-blooded man's dream."

"Oh, there's too many comebacks for that one." She lifted her arms like a set of weighing scales. "Manhood. Cold-blooded. You're just leaving yourself wide open."

Sebastian couldn't help but be amused by her. "I have an idea. How about you spread those legs of yours wide open, Ms. Diaz, and we can get this *ménage à trois* started?"

Isabella's laugh was wicked. It hit every nerve in his cock.

"My, my, aren't we eager?"

"I'm a man who knows what he wants."

"And that's me?"

"Clearly." Sebastian spread his arms wide, and Isabella looked down. Her mouth parted.

"How could I have missed that little detail?"

Sebastian inched closer, noticing the way she looked up from her long dark lashes. She was baiting him, and he was rising to the occasion. It baffled him why she got under his skin so much. For whatever reason, he was glad of it. The thrill of what was to come made him harder still.

"Trust me when I say there's nothing *little* about my detail, Isabella."

"That's what they all say."

Sebastian smiled at Rilla. "I get that you and this hellion had an arrangement, so I won't stand between you. But, if you're up for cock, then it's my civic duty to make myself available."

"I like him." Rilla grinned at Isabella, who rolled her eyes.

"Enough to let him stick his dick in you?"

"Trust me when I say there's plenty of dick to go around."

Rilla's smokey laugh was low and lusty. She winked at Isabella. "Oh, yeah. If he's just as cocky as he says, I'm game."

Isabella frowned, studying him for a second before looking away.

"Problem?" He cupped her hips.

"No."

"Good. Allow me to get you started then."

He watched her now, undoing the sash at her hips. Like her silk dress, the material was smooth, soft, alluring. Like the owner, it was a tantalizing call to his senses.

"Any objection if I use this?" He lifted the sash, winding it around his hands.

"Not at all. I'm usually up for anything, and trust me when I say, I'll let you know if I'm not keen."

"You? Outspoken?"

Her laughter tumbled out, rich and full.

"One point for you, Mr. Galvett."

"Let's settle the score at the end of the evening, Ms. Diaz."

Something sparked in her eyes. "I always win."

"We'll see about that."

He lifted the sash, covering her eyes with the material, breathing her in as he shifted closer to tie the bow.

"What did you have in mind?"

"Perhaps I should have used this to muzzle your pretty lips." He trailed a finger down from her top lip to her chin. He was about to do it again when she bit him. The sensation jumped straight to his cock.

"A tigress."

"I'm just hungry."

"Let's see if we can appease you."

Sebastian turned her to face Rilla, who, wasting no time, kissed her. Unable to help himself, he bit the curve of her neck.

He enjoyed hearing her gasp. He was enjoying a lot of things about her. Like the way her pulse thudded beneath his lips when he nibbled up to her earlobe. Or the way she cried out when Rilla squeezed her tits. They had all night to explore one another. To taste, experiment. He was going to use every minute like it was his last.

He unzipped her dress, trailing his finger down her spine. The silk whispered to the floor, a sensual heap, pooling around her heels.

"I only make one request." He murmured into her ear, watching her shiver.

"What's that?"

"Those heels stay on."

She grinned. "I think we can manage that."

When his hand undid the clasp of her bra, brushing the underside of her breasts, he fought not to squeeze and fondle. She had an amazing body: breasts ripe, hips flared, and legs for days.

"These need to go too."

He watched as goosebumps followed his fingers in feverish pursuit, around her back and down until it reached the birthmark just above the curve of her butt. It was a little crescent moon, no bigger than a fingernail. Next to it was a series of smaller marks—these all man-made—tattoos of tiny stars, a pattern of some sort of constellation. He traced it before pausing at the silk underwear.

Crouching down, his tongue followed the invisible line of his finger, first along the column of her spine, circling her mark, and then biting the scrap of red silk around her butt. He tugged her panties down with his teeth, breathing her in. He wanted to linger on her ass, to taste her pussy, but he forced himself to maintain control. That would come later.

He admired the pretty strap of her red and black heels, nipped the back of her knee, then switched to her inner thigh, feeding off her sighs. He didn't know if it was him or Rilla producing that reaction, and it spurred him on.

Not that it mattered. She would be a passionate lover, and tonight, he would take that fire, devour that energy in greedy bites until it satisfied whatever it was inside him that hungered. Whatever in him that remained cold and detached.

It was a part of himself that he accepted, fed, and down-right used as a fucking shield of armor for years now. But tonight, he would let go. A little. Feed off this infuriating, intoxicating woman and see just how sated he would be by morning.

Unable to stop himself, Sebastian traced the warm line of her snatch, hot and a little wet, drawing up past the thin landing strip on her pussy before licking the trail off his finger.

"You taste…just like you smell: sweet, of summer, oranges and blossoms."

"Wait until you bury your face inside her," Rilla murmured at her neck. "Like ambrosia. Hottest pussy in town."

"This so-called 'hot pussy' would like some attention." Isabella placed her hands on her hips, dark maroon nails flash-ing. Naked and blindfolded, she was a sight.

He nodded at Rilla. "Don't let me interrupt." Hard as rock and aroused beyond belief, Sebastian pulled away when all his senses told him to pounce.

He walked over to the stereo, forcing his stiff body to unwind, distracting himself with finding a tango song that would suit. He wanted it slow, heavy with anticipation, drip-ping with desire. Something that would consume them all.

Satisfied, he turned and watched as Rilla stood behind her, cupping Isabella's tits, tweaking her nipples until she gyrated. Those long, tattooed fingers inched lower, and in slow, seem-ingly torturous moves, she circled her clit. Isabella's head was thrown back, the delicate column of her throat exposed, her naked body on display. It was a sensual picture, one that would brand itself in his mind long after this was over.

There was something about Isabella's moans that beckoned. Something about her pleasure that drugged him, drawing him out of his own body and onto another plane of existence. He would lose himself in that body tonight.

"Join us, Sebastian."

He walked over to her slowly, fingers itching to explore. "I have something else in mind."

The beginning of a tango song floated towards them.

"May I have the pleasure of this dance?"

CHAPTER THREE

Isabella jerked as if burned.

Dancing. Naked. With Sebastian.

Her blood roared, bringing her out of the sexual spell.

It was overwhelming enough dancing with him at the *milonga*, but doing so stripped bare and blindfolded was madness. Images flashed. Hard muscle. Skilled hands. Sharp green eyes that were alert, always alert and…wary. It was like he was ready to pounce, to react to some unseen danger that lurked in the shadows. It had left her on edge over the years, but now she was simply curious.

What would she see if she lifted the blindfold?

"I won't say no."

"Rilla, do you dance?"

"Everyone does in this town."

"Wait." Isabella held up her hand. She could feel the smooth material of Sebastian's jacket under her palm. She had stipulations.

"You need to take off your shirt."

"Bargaining already, Isabella?"

"I know what I want."

"Very well."

She heard the rustle of material and a few seconds later felt the warmth of his body.

It was like stepping too close to the sun. Sandwiched between Sebastian and Rilla, hard and soft, stranger and lover, was almost too erotic.

Her nipples were sensitive, straining against his solid chest. Dancing in a semi-open embrace, Isabella grasped his arms, enjoying the sculpted muscle beneath her hands. She wanted to lift the blindfold and take a sneak peek at what he looked like, but instead let her mind wander.

Rilla's breasts brushed against her back, shadowing her movement. She was trapped, surrounded by warm bodies and wandering hands. The sweet, familiar scent of vanilla stroked her desire. Yes, this is exactly what she wanted. To lead and be lead.

They moved slowly, in small rocking steps, in time to the music. Sebastian displaced her foot, inserting his leg in between her naked thighs. The rough material of his trousers, the friction at her clit, sent shockwaves through her. Every step teased her arousal; every caress made her yearn for more. Faster. Harder. To be touched and fucked and devoured until she could barely breathe.

The contrast between them heightened her arousal; the unyielding and the supple. Hands and mouths exploring, feasting…her pulse quickened.

All the dichotomies of her body, all the needs she would normally cast aside would be fed tonight. She would be sated. For one night in this exotic, hedonistic city, she would exist without borders—for herself.

The tortured man before her would give her that. And she would take, take, take.

When the second song drifted across the room, Isabella let any residual reticence dissipate. Rilla's hands on her waist teased. She was more than aroused. She was captivated. And when something caught her attention, she pursued it with utter abandon. So she would throw herself in this moment, with this man and woman, and forget about everything else.

The tango wasn't fast, so they took their time. And in between slow circles of movement, she reveled in the way his hands travelled freely over her body. The delicious bubbles of energy that shot through her was exhilarating.

When the song came to an end, she tilted her face up then moaned when Sebastian's firm mouth descended on her own. He sent sparks flying through her body. How was it possible that a man so restrained was capable of this much passion?

While her mind whirled with possibilities, her body remained enslaved.

His tongue danced with her own, satisfying a need she hadn't known was there before. Not with him. But the kiss soon turned molten. She was caught in his net, his embrace, and still she demanded more.

When Sebastian pulled back, she tugged the ribbon from her eyes, searching his face. Beneath the façade, she saw the raw emotion, the clawing, driving need written across his face. It transformed him from a detached stranger into a compelling lover.

Damn him. Damn him to hell for making her want him. For being so intriguing. But most of all, damn him for doing it so fucking well.

"Just the two of you." His voice was raspy, thick. And

when he stepped away, she felt the absence across every inch of her body. She didn't care for the feeling one bit.

Sebastian sat on the armchair, making himself comfortable.

What was he playing at?

Isabella liked being on even ground. While she lived for the adventurous life, she conversely liked to know when she had people figured out. And for some infuriating reason, just when she had him pegged, he did or said something that threw out the impression she had made, leaving her on the back foot. She *hated* being proved wrong. But the arrogant, distant, moody stranger seemed to be doing just that.

Most men loved nothing more than being the center of attention in a three-way. At least, most of the men she knew. But here he was, happy to sit back, to watch.

The man was maddening, confusing…but damn it if he didn't intrigue her all the way down to her sexed-up core.

Isabella sought succor. Rilla offered it freely.

Swaying, they danced together, sampling each other as they had before, but everything was heightened. Rilla shoved her against the wide, exposed brick pillar. When she lowered to her knees, planting kisses down her stomach, her pulse jumped. She would never tire of this: the delicious expectation of a lover's mouth there. Right there. At her mercy.

She wanted to throw her head back, to close her eyes as the torrent of sensations flooded her clit, but the magnetic expression of the man across the room prevented her from turning away. She stared at him through heavy eyelids, desire a dizzying force, until a flush crept up across her body.

"Make her come," he said to Rilla. "I want to hear it."

She trembled, desperate now as the frenzy for release built

inside of her. The soft, wet tongue stroking her clit held her hostage. And suddenly she wanted movement. Needed to take charge.

She yanked at the short strands of hair until Rilla looked up.

"I'll be doing the fucking."

And just like that, the roles were reversed. Eager to come, Isabella led her friend over to the bed in the far corner of the room. Lifting up Rilla's short black skirt, she discarded her underwear and hovered over her. Straddling her now at an angle, she held Rilla's leg against her body then lowered down until her clit rubbed against Rilla's; the sensation nearly made her lose control.

She groaned instead, biting down on her slim ankle, working her hips back and forth.

"You like when I fuck you?"

"*Si.*"

"I bet you do." She looked up at Sebastian, still as a marble statue. "As for you, I'll say how and when I'll come."

"As you wish."

There was something about that deep rumble of his voice, the self-assured tone, which drove her a little wild.

Hips flying, she was caught between the soft, panting cries beneath her and the intense, enthralling gaze of the man across the room. In short, she was in heaven.

The soft, slick folds against her hot pussy was just the right amount of friction to get her off. She panted, letting it build and build until she couldn't hold back. With a satisfied cry, she let go, her orgasm sharp and sudden. Spent, she slumped against her, planting a soft kiss on Rilla's mouth, indulging in her soft, pliant body, now slick with sweat.

She brushed back her damp hair then looked up across the room at the man who watched in silence, green eyes hot, body still.

She was searching for something tonight. But it certainly wasn't *him*. Not here, exposed like this.

She had promised herself never to dance with Sebastian.

But sex was different. *This* was different. They weren't in a *milonga* but an apartment in the heart of Palermo, a stone's throw away from one of the hottest dance halls Buenos Aires had to offer. And they were naked.

She would never have agreed if she were back home. She wouldn't have succumbed to the intoxicating pull, that yearning deep in her belly. But they were in Buenos Aires, a place consumed by passion, and she was more than intrigued.

Despite her initial restraint, a baser, reckless part of her wanted him. To taste him. Feel him. Fuck him until she couldn't see his arrogant face.

Even if it was a damn hot one.

THE SILVER NEEDLE OF MOONLIGHT PIERCED THROUGH the windows. The oppressive heat clung to the air, mocking the whirring fan and its futility, one stroke at a time.

The cover of night didn't seem dark enough. Even here, with the candles low and strategically placed in the large center space, Isabella was still exposed. Beads of perspiration cradled her breasts. Her nipples strained in anticipation at what that mouth could do.

She wanted to rush, to devour and consume him whole,

but Sebastian built up her need until she was a stream of sensations.

"Time to have another taste of this pussy of yours. I hear it's particularly sweet."

He was at the foot of the bed, cock pressing against his trousers.

"I think there's something that needs taking care of, don't you, Isabella?" Rilla crawled over, unzipping Sebastian's trousers, freeing him from the barriers between them. He stood before her naked, exposed. She had to hand it to him, the bastard had an impressive physique: toned shoulders, sculpted biceps and a cock that was every inch as big as he had intimated.

"Looks like the man wasn't exaggerating." Rilla ran one finger along his shaft, and Isabella's mouth went dry. She wanted him to use that thick, hard length and pound into her until she couldn't think anymore.

Rilla lowered her head, taking him with mouth and hands.

Sebastian's groan filled the space between them, but his eyes never left hers. She toyed with her clit, then inserted one, two, three fingers, fucking herself, needing friction and contact.

"You mean you want to taste this snatch?" Isabella murmured, licking one finger, sticky and wet.

Sebastian's eyes raked over her body, hot and hungry. "You're a little tease, aren't you?"

"You're about to find out."

She kneeled behind Rilla and inserted her fingers in her pussy, stretching her, playing with her until she could take another finger, and another. Rilla's moans were muffled by Sebastian's cock.

Knowing she was ready, Isabella inserted her thumb until she was buried inside Rilla, pumping her with her fist, toying with that swollen clit.

"Fuck, that's hot." Sebastian's breathing was labored, and the sounds of them both lost in their own pleasure turned her on.

"Hot enough to come in her mouth?"

"Ladies first." Sebastian's hands were in Rilla's hair, guiding her. Isabella shoved aside the stabbing jealousy. She was greedy for his hands, his mouth, that cock.

Rilla rocked back against her, and moments later, the telltale squeezing around her fist began and Isabella picked up the pace. It wasn't long before Rilla came in hard jerking movements.

When she raised her head, Isabella shifted her aside, desperate for a taste. "My turn."

"You fucking tease. You know I'm close," Sebastian's voice was hoarse, his cock glistening.

"Tough."

Rilla's soft laughter floated around them. "I think you've met your match, McBroody."

Isabella was about to crouch down and take him in her mouth when she was pushed back on the mattress. He was suddenly above her, mouth claiming hers in a kiss that was frustration and desire rolled into one.

Sebastian yanked the pins loose from her hair, sending arrows of pain and pleasure down her spine. His fingers raked through her unbound curls as he penetrated her mouth, teasing and torturing her with his tongue.

When he eventually pulled back, Isabella bit down on her lip. She would not beg for more. Not a fucking chance.

Sebastian kneeled before her, his cock jutting, muscles strained. She forced herself to rise slowly when every bit of her wanted to pounce.

"I wanna come on those tits." He reached out to arouse, to tease. "You've a magnificent body, Isabella."

"Not before I have a taste."

"Be my guest."

And she did. With mouth and tongue, she sucked and licked. With small, satisfying nips, she tortured and then picked up the pace, delighted at his hands in her hair.

When she felt Rilla's tongue on her pussy, she knew she wouldn't last much longer.

"Fuck, you give good head. But I'm close."

And still, she didn't stop. She took the length of him deep, gagging and sucking until he gripped her hair and stilled, pumping into her mouth. Isabella sucked and swallowed, taking in the sweet, sticky cum until he groaned and pulled back.

"You can come on my tits later." Isabella wiped the corner of her mouth and smiled.

"I'll be coming all over your face for that."

Isabella shifted, placing a kiss on Rilla's lips, now damp. "We'll see."

Sebastian lay down on the bed. "And you'll be begging me before this is through."

"So you say." She crawled up his body, trailing her finger past the V of his abdomen, over the ridges and muscles and up to his mouth. "I don't beg for anything."

Sebastian slapped her ass. "We'll see. Sit on my face, you little tease, I'm tired of asking twice. And you—" He nodded to Rilla. "You can sit on my cock."

Isabella pressed her lips together, stopping the interjection before it embarrassed them all. She was *not* jealous. That would be fucking ridiculous. She didn't *do* jealous. And certainly not with Sebastian.

Rilla's moans beckoned, and Isabella glanced over her shoulder, watching as she lowered on Sebastian's cock, milking him with her lithe body.

"McBroody wasn't lying." Rilla's voice was low, breathless. "Fuck, Isabella, the man is built."

With a jerk of her shoulder, she turned back to see sharp green eyes assessing her.

She hovered over his face then looked down, heart slamming in her chest when he gripped her hips. Sebastian paused, holding her in place, an amused look in his eyes. She wanted to claw and scratch away that expression more than she cared to admit.

He teased her. Slowly, steadily, drawing out her need, making her body tremble. When his tongue lapped at her clit: small, quick strokes, every inch of her wanted to scream. He worked over her, and she couldn't help but rock her hips, playing with her tits, wanting it to never end.

Rilla's moans made her even wetter.

Sebastian gripped her ass, and before she could gasp, his tongue buried into her snatch. She was more than ready to be pounded, and the way he thrust in and out was a delicious foreplay, only heightening her desire for the main course.

Those capable hands inched up her body, squeezing her breasts, tweaking her nipples until she ground against his face. She fucked him, or he fucked her, she couldn't be certain. Isabella gripped the bed rail blindly, craving satisfaction.

She heard Rilla cry out, a sharp keening release and

suddenly she was coming, her own orgasm rushing through her, stealing her breath. She was lost in sensations, gloriously flying. Wonderfully alive.

She opened her eyes slowly, caught between satisfaction and fresh arousal. Coasting now, she inched down his body, thighs shaking, desperate to be filled.

He stopped her, hands cupping her face, drawing her close. "Rilla's right. You're just as sweet as she said."

She ignored the trembling in her body and looked behind her. Rilla lay at the foot of the bed, body flushed, eyes closed.

"Told you." Rilla murmured, mouth curving in satisfaction.

Isabella didn't know why that small gesture affected her so. It wouldn't do to focus on it.

Sebastian was hard and straining. His stamina suited hers perfectly.

Rising up, she hovered over him then thrust down, crying out. He stretched her in a way she hadn't expected.

"Like that?"

"Mhmm." She adjusted, taking as much of him in as possible. Isabella wasn't sure what it was she felt, but it spread across her skin, starting from their point of contact until it wrapped around her, squeezing past her protective barriers, infiltrating its way deep inside.

She wouldn't think about it. Wouldn't focus on it. Whatever it was, she wouldn't be fooled. It was way too easy to be led by emotions when it came to sex, and when it came to Sebastian Galvett, she couldn't be too sure.

Isabella pleasured herself, rubbing at her clit, feeling him hit the spot inside her that never failed to make her lose control.

When he gripped her hips, setting the pace, she let go. Slow, then fast, he took her closer and closer, only to draw back again.

Holding her close, he shifted to his knees, never breaking contact. He lifted one breast and sucked, feasting on her nipples. With every stroke, every bite, she was drowning further in her desire. His arms were bands of muscle holding her, his eyes blazed with need: Sebastian looked at her in a way she never thought possible.

Jesus, he was hot. All that dark hair, the strong, muscly body, wrapped around hers. She was in heaven. Or hell. She hadn't yet made up her mind.

He lay her back on the bed, and Rilla slid between them. She was caught between needing sweet release and wanting the pleasure to continue. Sebastian pounded into her while Rilla teased, building her desire until she thought she would go mad. Hands and mouths, tongue and teeth, she was a slave to it all.

She pulsed around his cock now, desperate, her body shaking.

"You're close. Come, Isabella. I can feel it."

"I—Sebastian."

"Now."

"Oh…I can't, I—" She could barely breathe from the force of it; she was lost, shaking, shattering into a million pieces as her orgasm tore through her. She sobbed, delirious, riding out the sensation. To be touched like this, utterly consumed, was more than she could take.

Before she could blink Sebastian reached his own climax, coming over Rilla's ass.

Again, the stab of jealousy pierced through her satisfaction. It ignited her temper. What the fuck was wrong with her?

She should be riding the afterglow. Coming down from the glorious orgasm she just had, not feeding the green-eyed monster. She couldn't be jealous of Sebastian and Rilla. It was mental. Ridiculous. And all too fucking real.

With her heart still pumping, Isabella shifted off the bed, stalking to the kitchen.

With shaking fingers, she opened the bottle of dessert wine and pulled out three glasses. Before she could do much more, a slender hand held hers. She stilled.

"Not for me, Isabella. I have a morning shift and the sun will be rising soon."

She turned to face Rilla, ignoring the relief that washed over her.

What. The actual. Fuck.

"Next time, then?"

Rilla nodded, placing a small kiss on her lips, before picking up her clothes and changing. The gentle click of the front door closing moments later seemed impossibly loud. She was alone. With Sebastian.

Isabella wasn't certain if the rolling sensation in her gut was more nerves or excitement. Neither reaction would do.

CHAPTER FOUR

"I CAN'T SAY I'VE EVER HAD A SEX BREAK BEFORE, BUT I think we might need it." Isabella walked back in with glasses and a bowl of fruit. Even though her movements were relaxed, there was an energy around her, an inferno of emotions. A lesser man would find it intimidating. He thought it was sexy as fuck.

"You're more of the love them and leave them type then?" Sebastian picked up a glass, watching the way she pulled up short, eyes flashing.

"I tend not to...linger."

"Consider this a sex intermission. Stamina is key if you're going all night, or morning." Sebastian amended, gesturing to the sky. They hadn't closed the blinds, and the inky darkness was giving way to a new day. "Sex parties aren't for the weak."

"Do this on the regular then, do you?"

"No...not anymore at least. But facts are facts, can't fuck if you're dehydrated."

"Marathon man?"

"Maybe. It's just bodies, empty vessels if there isn't a

connection. Even if it's just a shallow one. Not dissimilar to tango."

"The spiritual, the mental, it all aligns with the physical, doesn't it?" She sipped at the wine, then raised the glass to her flushed cheeks.

He liked watching her. The way her dark hair curled around her, wild and unbound, falling in every direction. She was like some exotic gypsy, a mystery to him. He gripped the glass. Hell, he didn't need any more of those in his life.

Sebastian cleared his throat. "It can. If you let it."

Isabella shook her head. "I would never in a million years have thought Sebastian Galvett would be attuned to the spiritual side of life."

He shrugged, absorbing the sting. "Believe it or not, I used to be."

"Connecting with the spiritual world and your body isn't something you lose. It's always there, Sebastian, whenever you're ready to reclaim it."

He was confused by her sincerity...confused by her in general if he was honest. Which is why he kept his guard up. Yet somehow, keeping his distance as they sat around talking, naked, seemed laughable. Impossible. Especially after all that explosive sex.

"Thanks."

"For what?"

"The reminder."

"What you mean is keep your damn opinions to yourself, Isabella?"

He stroked the arch of her foot, running his fingers from heel to toe. "There's too much that's happened for me to just simply let it all go."

"I wouldn't suggest you do that, just…" She pursed her lips, thinking. "Let it settle, heal a little bit instead of picking at the wound. You need to start somewhere."

"Easier said than done. And being open, being spiritual is…"

"Vulnerable?"

"Dangerous."

"Sebastian—"

"That tattoo on your back…constellations? You're into astrology?"

She nodded, eyes sharp, accepting his retreat. "Nothing escapes you, does it?" She smiled, indulging him. "I was born with that birth mark."

"The crescent moon."

He caught the frown, a mere flicker, before it disappeared. He realized it for what it was. Pain. He had seen that expression in the mirror too many times to count. Interesting.

"Yes. It reminds me that whatever pain I feel is small in comparison to the greater scheme of things. That mark is my connection to something bigger. I know it sounds wishy washy, but I'm interested in what makes people who they are, the events that define them. So I thought I'd add to my birthmark with a bit of astrology. It's the alignment of my star sign."

"And you think horoscopes can tell you about a person?"

"No…not entirely, but it affords people insights into their character, their behavior, what their preferences are like. Compatibility."

"Are we compatible?"

"I don't need to consult astrology or numerology to know the answer to that one."

Sebastian's mouth curved. "I'd agree with you there. However, we just had some pretty amazing sex. Or are you too proud to admit it?"

Her grin, when it came, was slow and wicked. "Not proud, no. Surprised."

"You thought I'd be a flop?"

She laughed then, and her eyes shone. "Honestly, I wasn't sure what to expect, but not a flop."

"How to damn with faint praise."

She was stunning. Sexy. Alluring. He wanted her with an intensity that scared him. It seemed he couldn't get enough.

"You're the opposite of a flop now."

He glanced down at his growing erection.

"Seems like the thing to do when I've a beautiful, naked woman in front of me."

"You think I'm beautiful?"

"You know you are. But yes, I do. And I want to take advantage of that, and you, before the day begins. If you're willing?"

"Asking my permission? Whatever have you done with Sebastian?"

"You must have spiked the wine."

"I don't need to drug any man."

"Or woman. Rilla a regular then?"

"She has been, but it's just a bit of fun. Something different."

"Anything goes in this city."

"Exactly. Sometimes it's easier to explore parts of yourself when you're not confined to your comfort zone, when you're a stranger. Buenos Aires is all about exploration, a city you can lose yourself in and I enjoy that."

It hit home, those words, her tone. There was something between them here. A soft, imperceptible relenting. The candlelight and the breaking of the dawn added to the illusion. It was enticing. And that scared the hell out of him.

"Sometimes you can be lost forever."

She shifted, sitting beside him now, her hand on his knee. "What happened?"

Sebastian shook his head. "I don't know. I still don't know. And it's killing me." He looked at her, couldn't stop himself from reliving those feelings, his inadequacy. "It was my fault. If it wasn't for what I did…" He rubbed his face, desperate to stop the memories. "Now she's gone."

"Seb—"

"No. You don't get it, Isabella. I was supposed to be there, and I wasn't. I let her down and now she's…"

"I shouldn't have asked. I—let it go for now. Leave it alone."

"I can't stop myself. I can't stop seeing her face everywhere in this cursed city. And I won't stop coming back. Isabella, I need to find out the truth. Even if it kills me, I need to know what happened."

"Give it time."

"It's been six fucking years of time. Of investigations. Of bullshit nothing answers based on bullshit leads. I want more than that. Zoey deserves more."

"She'll have it and you'll find those answers. I can feel it. But you can't give up hope, and you can't let it rob you of living."

Sebastian downed his wine and placed hers on the side table. "Speaking of living…"

He reached for her now, gentler, softer. Taking her beneath him, he kissed her, drugging them both, setting the flame alight until she trembled beneath him. When those nails raked through his hair, he shivered. Yes, this is what he needed. Wanted. He would have her again and again until he couldn't think anymore.

She opened her eyes, now shimmering with tears.

"No, Isabella." He kissed one corner, licking the lone tear that fell. "It's okay."

"Seb, I—"

"Let me forget. Isabella, help me to forget."

She dragged him down, mouth fusing to his. And those thoughts were forced back, back, back, into the depths of his memories. At least for today.

He let his senses guide him, let his arousal take hold. Sebastian nuzzled her neck, finding the spot that drove her a little crazy. She arched beneath him, writhing and gasping. He used his teeth now until he heard it.

"Please, Seb, please. Fuck me."

He inched back, and suddenly he was ravenous again. He wanted to lose himself inside her, bury deep in that warmth and let go.

"Begging, are we?"

Her mouth opened, eyes sharpening as she realized her error.

"Don't look so fucking smug."

"The thing is." He kissed her jaw. "I don't know what I'm more smug about." Then the tips of her breasts. "The fact that you actually begged." He bit at her nipple. "Or that I can drive you crazy enough to."

Isabella yanked his face down to hers. "Less talking. More

screwing. And if you ever mention it again, so help me God, you'll be blue-balled for a week."

The laughter that rang out of his chest felt good. "I think I can manage that."

He rubbed his hard cock along her clit, teasing and taunting her. Her hips shifted, jerking up off the bed.

He fingered her now, satisfied when she was slick and ready. Then he flipped her over on her stomach, kneading her round ass, alternating between bites and slaps until she was all but shoving her snatch in his face. He grabbed her half empty glass of wine off the table and poured it down her crack, letting it drip down onto the bed. He followed the trail, licking and sucking from her clit to her puckered hole, rimming her with his tongue before lifting her onto her knees.

He was far too ready to wait. Too impatient.

Spreading her cheeks, he guided his cock into her snatch and thrust, watching her ass hole tighten, feeling her pussy clamp down.

She was glorious, working him on her knees, rocking back and forth. Sebastian held her hips, pumping into her, his body caught in waves of pleasure. He stroked the line of her back, smacking one round cheek, enjoying her ass bouncing up and down.

Isabella clamped around him, rhythmically now until he thought he'd lose his mind. Drawing her back up against his chest, he gripped her breasts then played with her clit, feeling like he was going to explode.

He pulled out, breathing deep. He wanted to see her face when he came.

And then he stopped short. The golden light of dawn filtered through the window, kissing the tips of her dark hair, caressing the warmth of her skin. She was tousled and sweaty, her cheeks flushed, lips red. He'd never seen anything more stunning in his life.

Overwhelmed and suddenly uncertain, Sebastian lowered to her, kissing her with an intensity that summed up this new realization. He couldn't possibly like the woman. She was maddening and careless, bossy and stubborn.

But he wanted her with a possessiveness he had no right to claim.

She caressed his cheek, biting her lip. Those eyes were soft. Warm.

He covered himself now, and when he entered her again, it was suddenly different. Sebastian rocked in and out, just the tip, driving them both a little crazy, then thrust completely.

"Yes. Just like that."

With long, gliding thrusts, he built their passion. When she wrapped those long legs around his waist, locking him in place, a primeval, elemental energy took over. It made him feel like a man. She brought that out in him.

He surrendered. To her, that sensation.

And as the light between them grew brighter, he took them under. He drank in her sighs, feasted on her body, and gave them both the pleasure that they craved.

"Come with me, Isabella. I want to see you lose control."

"Together."

He hammered into her now, their bodies sweaty, skin flushed. His fingers moved to her clit, and she shook her head.

Taking her mouth, he devoured her in wild, fevered kisses, reveling in her moans.

"Sebastian! I'm—oh, fuck!"

The hard spasms around his cock signaled her release and

she arched up off the bed, body stiff as she shattered. He called her name as he came, emptying inside her, groaning in satisfaction as he did.

When his heart stopped racing, he pulled back and lay stretched out flat on the bed. She curled next to him, flushed, smiling, spent.

He had no words. And then he did. A question that had been plaguing him for a while now.

She watched him, waiting.

"Why do you hate me so much?"

Her dark eyes assessed him. Eventually she sighed, a soft sound coming from deep within her chest. He continued to play with the mass of curls at her temple, still wet from the night's exertions.

Isabella opened her mouth, but no sound came out. She tried again.

"I don't hate you."

"Anymore."

Her eyes warmed. "Let's just say it's downgraded to a mild loathing."

"I can live with that."

"I'm sure you've had worse." One dark eyebrow rose, a playful expression flittering across her expressive face. She was a striking woman. Everything about her screamed feline femininity. She had lost the dangly earrings somewhere along the way, but her exuberance, that colorful, loud way about her was there in every look, every comment.

He wasn't sure if he was intrigued or annoyed by it, but the feeling clamped around his reserves like a limpet in a rockpool. Like the sea, she was buoying, fierce and he suspected a little dangerous. Women like Isabella Diaz were warnings to men like him. A night of passion is all this would be. There wasn't room for anything more in his life, not if he wanted to find answers.

He didn't want to think about Zoey. *Wouldn't* think about her here. The grim circumstances of her death were too macabre for a night of licentiousness. He was a man who appreciated pleasure, just as he was one not to shirk from pain. Isabella seemed to offer both. He wasn't sure what to make of it.

As Sebastian succumbed to sleep, his body heavy, his mind free, the black chasm that echoed around him, accompanying his every move, dissipated a fraction. There was a light surrounding it now where there wasn't before. It held him close and comforted him in a way he hadn't felt in a long time.

Instead of being wary of it, he relaxed into what it might mean. For him. For her. For the future.

Hope.

WELL. FUCK.

Isabella watched Sebastian as his eyes grew heavy. Her own were nearly closed, but her mind whirled, robbing her of sleep.

Something had changed. She had felt it as sure as the daylight came in through the open windows.

He looked at peace like that. Asleep. He lost the cynical façade and instead appeared like any other hot guy, lost in a dream state. Except he wasn't. And she would do well to remember that.

Hell. She had the most amazing sex of her adult life with

the one man she loathed more than life itself. And she had no idea what to do about it.

Isabella bit her lip. She did loathe him, didn't she?

She tried to convince herself that nothing had changed. But Fate was telling her something different; the message pierced through her jumbled thoughts like the golden light of dawn, illuminating what had long been cast in shadow.

She wasn't sure she was ready to listen. Not yet at least. Maybe not ever.

The fortune teller's prediction from long ago floated down around her as she drifted off to sleep.

In her slumber, she reached for him. When Sebastian drew her in, holding her close, Isabella sighed, letting go of any lingering doubt. The prediction she had lived with for so long, once incoherent, and puzzling was now clear.

The answer lay beside her, if she was ready to accept him.

Want to read where it all began?
Then check out To Tango, with Love

ABOUT THE AUTHOR

Ida Brady writes contemporary romance novels that promise humour, heartbreak and a happily ever after. With all the sexy bits! A lover of chocolate (milk or dark) and thunderstorms (the bigger the better), she's usually dreaming about her next cast of characters or what she's going to eat for her next meal. When she isn't trying to tame her intractable curls, she's running after her kids, usually with a book in hand.

Ida lives in Melbourne with her Irish husband and their out-of-control collection of books. She sometimes daydreams about having a huge library in her apartment but will settle for stacking novels in the kitchen drawers instead. In her past life, she taught VCE Literature and English to a gaggle of teenagers. While she misses their enthusiasm, she sure as hell doesn't miss marking papers. You might find her dancing the sexy Argentine tango in her spare time, which isn't very often these days. She loves travelling with her family, observing strangers at cafés, and getting lost in a good story.

Visit: http://www.idabrady.com or sign up to her Newsletter, With You in Romance for giveaways and prizes!

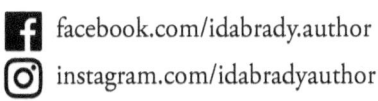

facebook.com/idabrady.author

instagram.com/idabradyauthor

ALSO BY IDA BRADY

To Tango, with Love

The Teacher Chronicles Series

Before You Were Mine

When You Were Mine (Coming 2022)

If You Were Mine (Coming 2022)

The Sweet, Sexy, Scandalous Series

Sweet Spot

Sex and the Stage

Secrets and Scandals

www.idabrady.com

ACKNOWLEDGMENTS

To my darling family, Team Brida. Brian, Adria, Niamh, and Hugo, I love you all to the moon, and back! Thank you for your understanding and patience. To all the members of my extended family, thanks for all the encouragement and support. Your interest in my work has motivated me more than you know.

To Christine (Christine's Cover Creations), for the wonderful work on my covers.

To Ebony McKenna, for your fab formatting and patience.

To Alessandra Torre, little did you know that your seminar unlocked the dormant idea for this series. It was the encouragement I needed without even knowing it at the time. Like all good ideas, this one wouldn't leave me alone until I had written it.

To Enticing Journey, for all your fantastic marketing and promotional work with this series.

To all the wonderful bloggers and reviewers who took the time to read my work, thanks for all the book love!

Once again, a big thanks to my tribe – the funny, whacky,

wonderfully inappropriate gang of the Romance Writers Meetup. I couldn't have asked for a more varied, encouraging, talented group of women to call my friends. I've really loved (and anticipated) our virtual chats and cannot wait until we can celebrate together in person.

To my BETA readers, once again, your time, effort and insight make me feel super lucky to have you all in my life. Thank you for all the feedback, encouragement, and support. Especially putting up with my short notice requests! Y'all ROCK!

Finally, to my readers. Whoever you are, wherever you may be, I hope that this novel gives you a chance to escape from reality, even if for a chapter or two.

With you in romance,

Ida Brady